Storm froze in disbelief. She hadn't fallen at all; she was on her four paws, in a turmoil of leaves and sand where she must have skidded and twisted. Her flanks heaved as she fought to control her desperate breathing.

Storm eyed the darkness around her. Spun on her haunches, and stared.

She was no longer in the camp. She was no longer in the glade. She was deep in the forest. And for the second time, she had no memory of how she had gotten there.

SURVIVORS

Also by ERIN HUNTER

WARRIORS

THE PROPHECIES BEGIN

EXPLORE THE
WARRIORS
WORLD

NOVELLAS

Hollyleaf's Story
Mistystar's Omen
Cloudstar's Journey
Tigerclaw's Fury
Leafpool's Wish
Dovewing's Silence
Mapleshade's Vengeance
Goosefeather's Curse
Ravenpaw's Farewell

SEEKERS

Book One: The Quest Begins
Book Two: Great Bear Lake
Book Three: Smoke Mountain
Book Four: The Last Wilderness
Book Five: Fire in the Sky
Book Six: Spirits in the Stars

RETURN TO THE WILD

Book One: Island of Shadows
Book Two: The Melting Sea
Book Three: River of Lost Bears
Book Four: Forest of Wolves
Book Five: The Burning Horizon
Book Six: The Longest Day

MANGA

Toklo's Story
Kallik's Adventure

THE GATHERING DARKNESS

SURVIVORS

A PACK DIVIDED

ERIN
HUNTER

HARPER

An Imprint of HarperCollinsPublishers

Special thanks to Gillian Phillip

A Pack Divided
Copyright © 2015 by Working Partners Limited
Series created by Working Partners Limited
Endpaper art © 2015 by Frank Riccio

For information address HarperCollins Children's Books,
a division of HarperCollins Publishers,
195 Broadway, New York, NY 10007.
www.harpercollinschildrens.com

Library of Congress catalog card number: 2015938992
ISBN 978-0-06-234335-2

Typography based on a design by Hilary Zarycky
18 19 20 BRR 10 9 8 7 6 5 4
❖
First paperback edition, 2016

For Fergus & Annie Nicol

PACK LIST

WILD PACK (IN ORDER OF RANK)

ALPHA:

female swift-dog with short gray fur (also known as Sweet)

BETA:

gold-and-white thick-furred male (also known as Lucky)

HUNTERS:

SNAP—small female with tan-and-white fur

BRUNO—large thick-furred brown male Fight Dog with a hard face

BELLA—gold-and-white thick-furred female

MICKEY—sleek black-and-white male Farm Dog

STORM—brown-and-tan female Fierce Dog

ARROW—black-and-tan male Fierce Dog

WHISPER—skinny gray male

WOODY—stocky brown male

PATROL DOGS:

MOON—black-and-white female Farm Dog

TWITCH—tan male chase-dog with black patches and three legs

DART—lean brown-and-white female chase-dog

DAISY—small white-furred female with a brown tail

RAKE—scrawny male with wiry fur and a scarred muzzle

BREEZE—small brown female with large ears and short fur

CHASE—small ginger-furred female

BEETLE—black-and-white shaggy-furred male

THORN—black shaggy-furred female

RUFF—small black female

OMEGA:

small female with long white fur (also known as Sunshine)

PROLOGUE

"What's wrong with him?" The little pup's whiskers shivered as she nudged the long grass fearfully with her nose. "I don't understand. What's wrong?"

Flinching back as her nerve deserted her, she pressed closer to her two litter-brothers. The other pup, the one who lay in the grass in front of her, didn't so much as stir. She could make out the hollow curve of his tiny flank through the green blades, but it didn't rise and fall with his breath. One small ear was visible too, but it didn't twitch, not even at the tip. She couldn't see the little pup's eyes, but some instinct told her she didn't want to, anyway. She trembled with uncertainty and fear.

One of her litter-brothers, the smaller one, cuddled tighter against her, and she felt the dampness of his wet nose against her ear. "He's sick, I think. Like Mother-Dog?"

The female pup shivered. Yes, Mother-Dog was sick. She hadn't been well since that fight they'd heard. Mother-Dog had crept under the house, telling the pups to leave her alone for a little while. That she'd be better soon. *But leave me be, pups.*

She'd been under the house now for a very long time. *Oh, Mother-Dog,* the pup thought with an inward whimper. *Aren't you better yet? It's taking so long . . . and now this pup is sick, and we don't know what to do. . . .*

"Perhaps we should wake the pup now," her litter-brother piped up. "Take him inside, where it's warm and safe?"

"I don't know if he'll wake up," she whined unhappily. "He looks so very asleep."

And there was something else, something she didn't want to put into words. As her nose twitched and she sniffed hesitantly, she caught it again: that odd tang, the one that made her shudder. It wasn't a proper dog scent. It wasn't how a pup should smell, she thought, bewildered. It was like old meat, like what the grown dogs had left behind uneaten.

"You're both being silly." Her other litter-brother, the largest of the three of them, sounded stubborn and squeakily gruff as usual, but even he couldn't hide the tremor in his voice. "We don't have to do anything. The Pack will be home soon. Alpha will make Mother-Dog better, and she'll make her own pup better too."

"Are you sure Alpha is coming back?" asked the smaller male pup hesitantly.

"Of course she is," the bigger one said with an air of superiority. He nodded toward the motionless little dog. "That's Alpha's pup. So she'll come back. See? Mother-Dogs *never* leave their pups."

"Oh." The littlest pup wagged his tail, hesitantly. "When she makes her pup well, maybe he'll play with us?"

This time the bigger pup said nothing, and neither did the female. She caught his anxious, uncertain look. That motionless pup didn't look as if he'd be able to play with them anytime soon.

Gathering her courage, she squirmed forward on her belly through the damp grass. It was nearly all she knew, this sheltering greenness. It had always been her whole world, and the sweet, fresh, familiar scent of it almost masked the pup's strange odor. She made herself creep closer till her quivering nose almost touched his flank.

She could just make out the bristly hair on the pup's neck. It looked stiff and dark, as if it had once been wet, and had dried a long time ago. Curious, she blinked. There were punctures, she realized, beneath those rigid prickles of fur. They looked a bit like the marks she and her litter-siblings had left on the soft-hide where they slept: ragged and torn at the edges. Their tiny teeth made those marks, she knew; chewing the hide gave them all comfort. But the marks here looked much bigger than that.

It didn't make sense. But she couldn't concentrate on working it out: the hunger that had nipped all day at her belly tightened, suddenly and sickeningly. She gave a low, miserable whimper.

"Don't worry," came her bigger litter-brother's voice again. "Everything will be fine when Alpha comes back." But he didn't sound so definite anymore. His voice quavered, as if he didn't quite believe it himself.

His new uncertainty made her belly twist with pain, and her ribs seemed to tighten around her heart. Throwing back her head, she gave in to a volley of high, yelping howls of fear and heartbreak.

"Mother-Dog is so still! The pup is cold! They won't move! Why won't they move?"

"Where's Alpha?" Her small litter-brother joined his miserable yelps to hers.

"There's no dog here!" she cried. "The food is gone and the Pack is gone. We're all alone and they've left us! *We're alone!*"

Now even her bigger, stronger litter-brother was howling his panicked grief. "They went away and left us, they've gone, they've all gone . . ."

Their high, frantic yips echoed through the grass and the trees and the sky, but she knew there was no dog in the whole world who would hear them. The awfulness of that thought filled her whole small being, and she could no longer stop her helpless crying.

Suddenly, though, she felt her bigger litter-brother's nose nudge her flank. "Hush!" he whined in a trembling voice. "Quiet, both of you. Some dogs are coming!"

At once all three fell silent, stiffening with a new, immediate fear. The female pup took gulps of air, trying to calm herself, trying not to whimper anymore. As she licked her soft jaws, she smelled them, too: unfamiliar dogs.

Strangers, and they were *coming this way.*

She glanced at each of her litter-brothers, seeing in their eyes the same mixture of hope and terror that she felt.

We're so alone . . . oh, Mother-Dog . . .

In sudden, desperate panic, the pups scrambled back to their soft-hide bed, climbing over one another in their haste. *The soft-hide is safe!* thought the female pup, as she wriggled between her

SURVIVORS: THE GATHERING DARKNESS

litter-brothers' paws. *Nothing can catch us there!*

They tumbled into the bed, panting. In its familiar-smelling warmth, they huddled together. She pressed her empty belly tight against the soft-hide, knowing she had to stay down low. She was too afraid to look. She mustn't make a sound, not a sound. Mustn't twitch . . .

Maybe they'll help. Don't dogs help pups? They always do . . . right?

Something awful, something long lost, trembled in the depths of her memory, and she shut her tiny eyes tight.

Or maybe they'll kill us. . . .

CHAPTER ONE

Pausing as she stepped out of the forest's shade, Storm took a moment to stretch her paws and her back, and to claw the ground blissfully in the rays of the morning Sun-Dog. His light shone warm on her sleek fur and, in the rippling grass around her, he kindled rich scents of rabbits, mice, and squirrels. Storm sniffed appreciatively at the soft breeze. There were good prospects for their hunting patrol.

Storm felt full of optimism on this glittering New Leaf day. It was her first chance to be in charge of a hunt, and she was proud that her Pack Beta, Lucky, had shown such faith in her. *He always has,* she thought gratefully. She owed so much to the golden-furred Beta who had once been a Lone Dog.

She glanced over her shoulder at the team she was leading. *Some of the Pack's best dogs,* she thought with pride. Snap, who had long been part of Sweet's Pack, had always been a fine hunter, and Mickey, despite his Leashed Dog origins, had learned to track down prey with the best of the Wild Dogs. Arrow the Fierce Dog had been one of Blade's Pack, and his focus, discipline, and deadly accuracy were invaluable assets. And Whisper, who had been one of the mad dog Terror's underlings . . . well, he was extra keen to please his leaders and prove his worth, now that he wasn't cowed by Terror's horrible threats.

They were an unlikely combination, but that was what made Storm happiest. Before her own birth, the Earth-Dog had shaken in the Big Growl. If that had never happened, the Packs represented in her hunting party would never have come together as one. After all, Mickey and Snap had come from very different circumstances—Snap from Sweet's Pack, which had once been the half wolf's Pack; and Mickey from his home with longpaws—but that was before the Big Growl had destroyed the city, changed the world, and forced every dog to fend for himself. Now they all worked together despite their differences, all of them bringing their own strengths and skills to their new, united Pack.

Storm had never quite understood why Lucky was always barking back to the Big Growl. Yet now that she had lived through a great battle—the one they called the Storm of Dogs—she saw clearly why the disaster of the Growl meant so much to him. When a dog had lived through such a world-changing shock, it did affect everything: the world beneath her paws, the scents in her nostrils, each sound that reached her pricked ears. Everything held new significance—and not just potential threat and unexpected danger, but fresh possibilities, too.

Prey had been thin and hard to catch throughout the long Ice Wind season, but now buds were popping into life on the trees, small leaves grew thick on the bushes and shrubs, and the meadows were green with new life. Storm was determined that today's hunt would be swift and successful. "Try that hollow, Storm." Mickey's kind voice was in her pricked ear, and it set her fangs instantly on edge. He and Snap had been trying to advise and guide her all morning, when it was Storm herself who needed to make the decisions. Couldn't Mickey understand that?

"There, see?" the black-and-white Farm Dog went on, oblivious as Storm ground her jaws in frustration. "The hollow beyond the hill." He nodded in the direction of the far side of the shallow valley, toward a dip in the grassy ground circled by young birch saplings.

"Yes, that might be worth a try," Storm managed to growl.

"We can surround it easily and drive out the prey," Mickey

went on. "The creek runs close to it, and there's a rabbit warren there."

"I know that, Mickey," said Storm sharply.

Mickey pricked his ears in surprise, then licked his jaws. "Did I say something wrong, Storm?"

"It's just that—" Noticing the slight hurt on his face, she softened, and gave her old friend a lick. "Sorry, Mickey. I'm just a bit preoccupied."

He was only trying to be helpful, after all—and Mickey, along with Lucky, had been one of the dogs who had rescued her and her two littermates when they were helpless, abandoned pups. He'd always looked out for her.

But I want to be able to prove myself. *If they'll let me . . .*

Snap was the next to trot over and push her narrow snout in. "I'm not sure about those high trees, Storm." Her head tilted as she stared at the horizon. "Rabbits could duck around them, and we'd be blocked at several points."

Storm somehow managed to hold on to her temper, though the urge simply to run and hunt was growing unbearable. Her paw pads ached, as if she'd been walking over rough stone, and she wanted to be moving now, not standing still. She could already see distant tawny flashes through the grass. The unwary creatures weren't alarmed—yet—but the dogs would have to move quickly once they were nearer to the warren.

"I think we can cope with the trees, Snap," Storm told her in a low voice. "Let's head toward the hollow, but keep our noses sharp for other prey on the way. We can't rely on catching enough rabbits for every dog."

She reminded herself sternly that Snap and Mickey were her seniors in the Pack hierarchy. *Though I wish they didn't treat me as if I'm still that vulnerable pup Mickey and Lucky rescued.* She gave a silent inward sigh, then nodded at her patrol.

"I want to plan ahead of time, so that we don't have to make a sound later. Arrow and Snap, when we're closer to the warren, you circle around toward the creek. If the rest of us take points between the warren and the wider plain, the rabbits will have nowhere to go. We should manage to take two or three. Stay low, and remember to watch for other prey." With a nod that Storm hoped showed both respect and quiet authority, she led the patrol carefully toward the line of aspens on the horizon.

All the dogs were alert now, placing their paw pads with care and keeping their bodies low, but Whisper slipped past the others to stalk at Storm's side. She gave the young dog an inquisitive glance.

"I think this is a brilliant strategy, Storm," said Whisper, in a low but enthusiastic growl. "You're a great hunt leader!"

"Thanks, Whisper," Storm told him, pricking her ears in slight surprise. "I'd really like to lead the hunt more often, so let's hope this goes well."

"Oh, I'm sure it will. So what else do you think we'll find? Maybe a deer!"

Storm gave a huffing sound of amusement, and shook her head briefly. "I doubt we'll be that lucky, but let's stay alert."

"You always do," said Whisper. There was a light of adoration in the gray dog's eyes, and Storm looked away, trying to keep her focus on the careful stalk-and-slink of the hunt.

A ripple of unease traveled between her fur and her skin. Whisper had treated her with something close to hero-worship ever since Storm had killed Blade, the Fierce Dogs' vicious leader, in the great battle last Ice Wind. Storm had had to do it—and she'd been glad to do it, after all that Blade had done to her litter-siblings and to her Packmates—but the days of battle were over. She was a hunter now.

She hoped Whisper wouldn't always be bringing up the dreadful Storm of Dogs, and Storm's role in it. They had a new life to look forward to now, and Storm was determined to play her part in making it one of peace and plenty for the Pack. It had taken her so much time and effort to live down her reputation as a savage Fierce Dog, a struggle made far harder by the hostility of their old half-wolf leader, Alpha. She didn't want to have to go through all of that again.

Storm raised her muzzle to test the wind direction, pausing with one paw lifted.

Forest-Dog, if you'll listen to me as you listen to Lucky, grant us good New-Leaf prey today!

Her optimism returned as she leaped easily over a small tributary of the stream, enjoying the sleek movement of her muscles and the springiness of the earth beneath her paws. Every sense in her body felt awake after the long, hard Ice Wind, and a slight flash of movement at the corner of her eye sent her twisting in pursuit almost without a thought.

The squirrel shot up the trunk of a tree, panicked, but Storm's snapping jaws found their target. Crunching down, she felt the brittle bones of its body through the scrawny flesh. *Skinny,* she thought, *even for a squirrel. Ice Wind has been hard for every creature.*

Her swift kill, she realized, had served as a signal to the others: the hunters bolted into the chase. Arrow sprinted across a dry streambed, sniffing and searching without luck, but Mickey and

Snap began to work together at the foot of a gnarled oak, digging in showers of earth until their paws and muzzles were filthy. Just as Storm bounded to join them, they unearthed a nest of mice. As the tiny creatures skittered in panic, blinded by the light, the two hunters pounced and bit and snapped till they'd created a pile of tiny corpses.

"They're barely a mouthful each," said Snap, pawing at them.

"Every mouthful feeds the Pack," Storm reminded her, pleased. "Well done!"

Her praise, though, seemed to fly straight above Snap's head. The tan-and-white dog pressed her head to Mickey's, and for a moment the two successful hunters rested, panting, rubbing their muzzles affectionately together and licking each other's dirty ears. With a surprised prick of her own ears, Storm took a few paces backward.

Is this really the moment for snuggling up to your mate? she thought with a shiver of puzzled distaste. *What a silly waste of time. It's only a couple of mice, for the Sky-Dogs' sake.*

Turning her rump on them, she snatched up her squirrel and dropped it into the hole Mickey and Snap had dug out at the base of the oak. It was as good a place as any to store their prey till they'd finished their hunt: a deep gap between two thick roots. As she raised her head, a light, warm breeze moved through the trees, bringing with it that tantalizing scent of rabbit. Storm shook off her moment of discomfort. *We're downwind of the prey—this is a good beginning!*

Excitement rose in her once again, and she gave a low commanding growl to summon the others. She felt a spark of pride, swelling to a warm glow, when they answered her call at once. The four dogs fell in at her flanks and followed her lead as she prowled forward, closer and closer to the shallow bowl of land.

The rabbits must be hungry after the long cold, Storm realized: they had still not noticed the patrol's approach. They were too busy browsing and tearing at the new grass with their blunt little teeth. *We should be able to cut them off from their burrows*, thought Storm, *if we all play our part.* Her heart beat fast in her rib cage with anticipation.

Lowering her sleek body still closer to the earth, she crept forward, nodding to the others. They were all in place, just as she'd directed them; again she felt that frisson of satisfaction in her leadership. When she finally sprang, hurtling into the hollow, every nerve in her body sang with the joy of hunting, with the certainty of her own speed and strength and skill. She felt her blood racing, the flex and stretch of each muscle as she dived and dodged and leaped in pursuit of the terrified rabbits. It was like pure energy and fire running through her. *Is this how Lightning of the Sky-Dogs feels?*

And it was working just as it should. White bobtails flickered all around the hollow, and the panicked creatures were scattering straight into the jaws of the waiting hunters. Mickey's powerful teeth clamped down on one of them, and he shook it violently as another doubled back and fled from him—straight into the jaws of Storm. Panting, Storm flung down its limp corpse, then took a moment to watch as Whisper drove the fattest rabbit of all toward the waiting Arrow.

Arrow was loping along on exactly the right line, and Storm could see he would intercept the fleeing rabbit with ease. So she was stunned to see Whisper's head flick to the side. Mid-stride, he veered away slightly and herded the rabbit in a different direction, toward Snap.

But Snap wasn't watching; she was too busy chasing down a dark-furred rabbit of her own. Whisper's rabbit crossed her field of vision just as she was about to pounce on hers, and Snap's pace faltered in surprise and confusion.

Arrow was racing furiously after the rabbit now, but the abrupt change of tactics had spoiled his line and his focus. Both rabbits, the dark-furred one and the lighter one Whisper had been driving, bolted straight between Arrow and Snap, and vanished into their burrows with a flash of two white tails.

Storm raced toward them, but she knew she was already too late. Skidding to a halt in a flurry of sandy earth, she stared at the dark burrow entrances, swamped by frustration and anger. Behind her, Arrow and Snap had drawn up too, snapping their drooling, empty jaws.

As Whisper bounded to a faltering, shamed halt between them, Storm turned on him.

"Why did you do that?" she barked furiously. "We lost two good rabbits!" *And more*, she realized. In the confusion of Whisper's mangled hunting attempt, several other rabbits had reached the safety of their warren.

"That was the fattest rabbit!" added Arrow in an angry snarl. "Those two would have fed three dogs between them!"

"What were you thinking? Were you thinking *at all*?" Storm laid her ears back and growled furiously at Whisper.

The dog ducked his head, lowering his forequarters and shuffling forward, his tail clamped down tight. He looked as if he wanted to sink right through the earth and join the rabbits underground.

"I'm sorry, Storm," he whined miserably, blinking and flattening his ears. "I didn't mean to . . . I thought . . . I just meant . . ."

Storm gave her head a violent shake. "*What?* What did you mean?"

"I—" Whisper's glance flicked quickly toward Arrow, then back to the ground.

"Don't be hard on him, Storm." Snap took a pace forward, and nodded at the unhappy Whisper.

Storm turned to her, surprised at the hunt dog's tolerance. "He spoiled your hunt too, Snap."

"Look, Storm, it's obvious." Snap tilted her head and sat down, curling her tail around her haunches. "Whisper was nervous of Arrow. He doesn't like hunting with him, and to be honest? I understand why. I don't blame Whisper."

Storm stared at Snap's cool expression, her jaw loose. "What?"

"After all we went through with the Fierce Dogs, it's hard for us to trust any of them." Snap hunched her thin shoulders. "I know Arrow's in our Pack now, but it's hard to treat him as a true Packmate."

Not knowing what to say to that, Storm turned to Arrow. His short black fur bristled along his shoulders and spine, and resentment oozed from him, but the Fierce Dog said nothing. He licked his jaws angrily, and looked away. Then he padded across to one of the dead rabbits, picked it up in his powerful jaws and paced in the other direction.

And what do I do now? Snap wasn't being fair, and this felt so wrong to Storm. *Just when I was thinking how good it was that we were united, that members of all Packs were working together.*

But if she spoke up for Arrow, Snap would think she was only siding with her fellow Fierce Dog. She might even accuse Storm openly of favoring her own kind, of being Fierce Dog to her core. *What might she say aloud—that I'm ruled by my bad blood?*

"You all trust me," she said at last, staring at her Pack-mates. Snap, Mickey, and Whisper looked so resolute, and Storm's head spun with confusion. "You trust me, and I'm a Fierce Dog too. Just like Arrow!"

Mickey caught Snap's eye, and Storm saw a look pass between them, one that she couldn't quite read. Snap's ear flicked once, dismissively. Then, tentatively, Whisper gave a soft growl.

"You're not like Arrow," he mumbled. "You're different." He glanced at Snap and Mickey. "Storm's different, isn't that right? She killed Blade!"

Storm stared at him, open-jawed. With a crawling sense of

horror, she realized that Whisper's eyes were fixed on her again, worshipful.

She shook herself, dumbfounded. "Let's gather the prey," she told them. "What there is of it." Gazing dismally at the pitiful haul of rabbits, she felt a crushing sense of disappointment. Her hopes had been so high for her first time as hunt leader. "We'll try another spot before we return to the camp, but we'll have to go some distance. All the prey around here will have heard us by now."

"Of course, Storm." Whisper got quickly to his paws and trotted after her like a devoted pup.

As she led the small patrol farther from the cliffs and the Endless Lake, heading for a far belt of pines, Storm's stomach squirmed and her fur prickled. She'd begun this hunt with such high hopes and excitement, yet now they were returning with a poor prey-haul—and a bunch of dogs who didn't, after all, want to work together as her perfect team.

Is that terrible battle the only thing they care about? If I hadn't killed Blade, would they trust me at all? Or would I be just another Arrow—alone in a Pack that thinks I'm the enemy?

CHAPTER TWO

Hungry as Storm was, the rabbit dangling from her jaws didn't even tempt her as she led the hunting party back to the camp. Her paw pads hurt, more than she thought they should, and her appetite was dampened by the sinking sense of failure in her gut. The dogs had tried their luck at a few more likely spots, but the rabbit warren in the hollow really had been their best chance, and by the time the Sun-Dog was loping down the sky, they had caught little more: a gopher, a couple of voles, and a skinny rabbit Storm suspected had been ill anyway.

Long shadows lay across the camp by the time they returned, making golden stripes through the trees that glinted on the freshwater pond. Storm's heart lifted a little as she carried her rabbit to the prey pile beneath the two trees in the camp's center. Bella had taken out another hunting patrol and they'd come home with their own catch—not much better than Storm's, but together the two patrols had found enough to feed all the dogs. Storm felt a tide of relief; at least her first day leading a hunting patrol wouldn't end with a hungry, discontented Pack.

Across the glade she could make out the golden shape of Lucky, sprawled with his mate—the Alpha, Sweet—and the white-and-black Farm Dog Moon. The three senior dogs were talking softly, but their conversation couldn't have been too serious because Lucky rose to his paws as he caught sight of Storm. He stretched lazily, then padded across to greet her, giving her an affectionate lick on the jaw.

"Well done, Storm," he told her, pricking an ear at the prey pile, where the other members of her party were already dropping their catch. "Your first hunt seems to have gone pretty well."

The rabbit in her mouth immediately tasted more appealing. "Not bad," she murmured through its flesh, glancing away a little. "Could have been better."

"It was a good first hunt for a new leader, take my word for it." Lucky nuzzled her reassuringly, but she saw that his dark eyes were distant, already drifting back to Alpha. The slender swift-dog was not so lean anymore: her sides were rounded with her and Lucky's pups, and even as Storm watched, their Alpha shifted position and stretched her hind legs as if she was uncomfortable. Lucky's gaze was a combination of love, pride, and faint anxiety, and Storm felt a prickle of fondness for him, even as she cocked one ear in bewilderment. *Is it really that exciting? I know they're his first pups, but hunting's got to be a lot more fun than fatherhood.*

He was obviously distracted, so Storm sidled away and padded to the prey pile herself to lay her rabbit on top. The little twist in her stomach was odd. It was right that Lucky should be focused on Alpha now, and on their soon-to-be-born pups. He'd be a wonderful Father-Dog, that was obvious—and Storm knew it from experience. He'd helped to bring her up after he and Mickey had found her and her littermates abandoned, and she'd never stop being grateful for Lucky's kindness, his bravery in defending her, and his constant good advice.

But she was almost fully grown now. She was an adult dog, or very nearly, and she didn't depend on Lucky anymore. She *shouldn't*, Storm reminded herself.

And it's not as if Lucky is my real Father-Dog.

Shrugging off her confusion, Storm glanced around for a friendly Packmate to while away the time with before prey-sharing. She was glad to spot Moon's nearly grown pups Thorn and Beetle, tumbling on the ground in a play-fight. As she padded up to them, Thorn took her teeth out of Beetle's ear and bounded up to her, yelping a cheerful greeting. "How did your first hunt go, Storm?"

"It was fine," she said, still a little reluctant to talk about it, and the worries it had stirred inside her about her role in the Pack. Quickly she added, "What about your patrol?"

"All quiet," barked Thorn, shaking her muscles loose after her tussle with her brother. "Except for a trace of fox, but it wasn't very new. We're not too worried."

"Hah!" Beetle nipped affectionately at her muzzle, then bared his impressive teeth. "No fox had better dare come near this camp, or there'll be a new fox-hide bed for Alpha and her pups!"

"You're all jaw," yapped Thorn. "Any fox *you* could catch would only have a skin big enough for one milk-pup."

"Is that so?" With a growl of laughter, Beetle twisted and pounced back on Thorn's haunches, dragging her down and tumbling her over and over till both dogs were covered in sandy earth and dry leaves. Thorn ended up on top, though, and she grazed her teeth along her litter-brother's exposed belly.

"See? All talk!"

With a swift and tricky squirm Beetle flipped her over again. "Storm, help me teach my litter-sister some manners!"

Yelping with glee, Storm piled into the play-fight, gnawing and snapping lightly at both pups. All three were soon wrestling and tumbling in a chaotic heap of legs and bodies. Beetle's paws shoved her down into a pile of leaves, but Storm wriggled free and grabbed his neck in her jaws, sending them both thudding to the ground—with Thorn pouncing on top of them, yapping her triumph.

"Oof!" barked Storm hoarsely. "Why are you two so fat after Ice Wind?" She felt almost giddy with happiness, with the sheer fun of acting like a pup again. *Maybe not quite fully grown, then,* said a cheerful small voice in her head.

"Fat, eh?" Thorn clamped her jaws around Storm's. "I'll—"

"Prey-share!" Alpha's clear, commanding bark rang out through the glade, and all three young dogs paused in their tussle, ears pricking. "To me, Pack."

Getting to their paws, Storm, Thorn, and Beetle shook themselves free of earth and leaf scraps and shared a few friendly licks. But Storm noticed both the other youngsters tense as they stared at the spot where the Pack was gathering.

Thorn's eyes narrowed. "Twitch had better not try to eat before our Mother-Dog," she growled, and Beetle nodded grimly.

Storm pricked her ears, surprised. The play-fun had gone out of the young dog's voice entirely. Thorn wasn't joking.

"I'm sure Twitch wouldn't do that," Storm reassured her. "Anyway, what does it matter?"

"Twitch has been getting above himself lately," rumbled Beetle, with a glare at the three-legged dog. "Our Mother-Dog outranks him, and he'd better not forget it."

Storm gave a sigh, but kept her jaws shut. *Who cares, so long as every dog eats?*

With a slight hunch of her shoulders she trotted ahead of Beetle and Thorn to join her Packmates. They were all settling into their circle, lying or sitting with their friends and littermates. Every dog watched with respectful affection as Alpha nosed the prey pile, selecting a modestly sized rabbit and carrying it back to her place.

It was a sparing choice, thought Storm admiringly, for a soon-to-be Mother-Dog. *Enough to feed her and her unborn pups, but not too much. She's a thoughtful leader as well as a strong one.*

Lucky was next, as Pack Beta. Like Sweet, he took a reasonable but not greedy portion, choosing a smaller rabbit. When he had settled back at Sweet's flank, the Alpha nodded to her third-in-command.

"Go ahead, Snap."

The sleek lead hunter nodded and stepped forward, but Storm

couldn't help but notice the tension that rippled through some of the Pack. *Twitch's former comrades*, she realized. There seemed to be an undercurrent running through those dogs, an unseen force she could feel, like the frightening pull of the deepest part of the river. Storm flicked her ears nervously. One of Twitch's former Pack growled softly, but no dog reacted, and none said a word.

After Snap, the hunters were summoned in strict order of rank. Storm felt proud to be called in the middle of them, and she was careful to follow the example of Sweet and Lucky, selecting a modest half of one of the rabbits she'd caught. She felt even prouder when Mickey, the steadfast Farm Dog, growled to her quietly as she passed him.

"Sensible choice. And well done on your catch, Storm. A good hunt!"

She lifted her head higher as she resumed her place in the circle, her belly comfortably full, her heart light with happiness. It felt good to be respected for more than her part in a violent, bloody battle; to be appreciated for what she could bring to the Pack's day-to-day existence.

The hunters of Twitch's Pack ranked below the original hunters of Sweet's Pack, and Alpha let them wait almost till the end—only Arrow, the lowest-ranked hunter, who had been one of Blade's Pack, was left to follow them. Woody, Whisper, and Breeze fidgeted and muttered among themselves, looking agitated, and when it was his turn, Woody glanced hesitantly toward Twitch, as if waiting for his former Alpha's permission to eat. Twitch said nothing, however, and when Sweet prompted Woody again, he stepped up to the prey pile. Whisper looked relieved that the awkward moment had passed—but Breeze glared sullenly at the dogs of Sweet's original Pack. A nervous tingle unsettled Storm's back fur, and she felt a creeping sense of unease.

"Patrol dogs next," announced Alpha, turning her warm gaze on the dogs who came below the hunters in the Pack hierarchy. "Twitch?"

The buzz of tension instantly intensified, as if Lightning had leaped from the sky and run unseen through every dog. Storm glanced around, alarmed. Moon's hackles were bristling, though she said nothing; Thorn, on the other hand, gave a single angry yelp. Beetle's low growl was hostile.

"My Mother-Dog Moon has always led the patrol dogs," he grumbled.

Beetle, shut up, thought Storm, nervous and angry. *What does it matter? Can't you see there's enough for every dog? Sweet and Lucky made sure of that!*

Twitch took no notice of the tension in the atmosphere, but simply limped up to the prey pile, silent and dignified. Alpha turned her elegant head to stare at Beetle, then at his litter-sister Thorn.

"Your Alpha makes the decisions here," she said sharply. "Remember the Pack."

When Twitch finished eating and returned to his place, Moon stepped up. The two dogs did not look at each other.

Storm was relieved when at last the meal was over, when Sunshine the Omega had gulped down the two little mice that were left for her. Sharing the prey had been an unnerving experience tonight. Though every dog had eaten, none seemed satisfied, and each dog shifted and scratched with nervous energy.

Storm got to her paws and turned to Beetle and Thorn, dipping her head slightly and letting her jaw fall open in a friendly grin. "Play-battle some more?"

"I don't think so." Thorn's growl was stiff, and Beetle shook his head and turned away to nibble angrily at his flank.

Rebuffed, Storm paced uncertainly among the small groups of dogs who were curling up to murmur among themselves. None of the conversations seemed very high spirited, and any excitement in the evening had been dampened by the awkward prey-sharing.

Ducking her head, Storm glanced surreptitiously at Lucky and Sweet, nestled against each other on the highest patch of ground. They looked as much on edge as any other Pack dog.

Alpha stretched and rose to her paws, gazing around at her Pack. "I think now would be a good time for a tale of the Spirit Dogs."

One or two of the Pack grunted sullenly, but most looked relieved to have their minds distracted. Little Sunshine gave a yelp of determined enthusiasm, wagging her bedraggled white tail. "I'd like that!"

"So would I." Mickey lay down, forepaws extended, and gazed expectantly at Sweet.

Alpha shared a glance with Lucky, whose tail thumped encouragingly. "Shall I tell you about the Wind-Dogs?" she asked.

"Yes! I love hearing Spirit Dog stories!" Daisy the patrol dog panted happily.

Moon looked puzzled. "But I've never heard of any Wind-Dogs," she growled.

Twitch tilted his head curiously. "I think I might have," he said, "but it was a long time ago. I don't remember anything about them."

"Well." Breeze stood up on all four paws, wagging her tail as her tongue lolled. "The Wind-Dogs sound good to me! Especially with my name!"

Alpha nodded. "Then I'll tell you who the Wind-Dogs are, and how they move through our world as silent and swift as the breeze." She blinked at Breeze, who pricked her ears in pleasure.

"Of course, they are the fastest of all the Spirit Dogs," Alpha went on, lifting her slender head so that every dog could hear her. "That's why the Wind-Dogs watch over swift-dogs like me and the members of my birth Pack."

"But what do they do?" yapped Daisy.

"Sometimes they hunt the Fastest Hare, a mischievous creature who once tried to trick them, and whose family must now run from us swift-dogs forever. But mostly they chase after the Golden Deer. They hunt her across the world, from forest to lake, over cliffs and plains and mountains. You can feel the breeze as they pass—sometimes so fast they leave destruction in their wake. Sometimes they run idly, loping gently along, and the wind of their passing is soft and soothing. But as they run, they take the world from warm to freezing cold, and back again. When Long Light ends, we know that they have caught the Golden Deer at last. But the Deer rises and runs again at the end of Ice Wind, and we feel the world grow warm once more."

Daisy gazed up at her Alpha, awestruck. "So the Golden Deer has begun to run again now," she said dreamily.

"Oh, yes. She's running now, on her long course through the world toward the next Ice Wind." Alpha cocked her head fondly at Daisy. "But she will run for a long time first. She is fresh and fast, and the Wind-Dogs have only just begun their new chase."

Sleepily, Storm settled herself against Thorn's flank. Even Moon's two youngsters had fallen under the spell of the story, and the tension had drained from their bodies. Storm could feel Thorn's calm heartbeat through her rib cage, and suddenly all seemed well. Once again, she could feel like a pup, safe and secure with the adults of the Pack.

Martha used to tell us stories, she remembered with an aching sadness. *She'd tell Grunt and Wiggle and me all about the Spirit Dogs. We didn't know anything, because our Mother-Dog died before she could tell us.*

But Martha was my Mother-Dog, too, really. Lucky and Mickey had raised her too, but it had been Martha, the huge and gentle black water-dog, who had come closest to replacing her lost Mother-Dog. She had comforted Storm when she was only a helpless pup called Lick; she had shared the warmth of her body, consoled her, protected her from the hostility of the other Pack members.

I miss Martha. . . . When she died, it was like losing my Mother-Dog for a second time.

Alpha's voice penetrated Storm's wistful thoughts, and she was glad. "Only the Wind-Dogs may hunt and capture the *true* Golden Deer, who runs free through every forest. But she casts a shadow. And if we run hard and run fast, we can catch that shadow, a living Golden Deer, as the real one races on into the sky. That's when a Pack is truly blessed by the Spirit Dogs."

Storm liked this story. *I'll catch a shadow of the Golden Deer one day. And when I do, I'll remember to thank the Wind-Dogs for it. I never knew about them before. . . .*

It was odd, yet strangely reassuring, to know that the swift-dogs had stories of their own, stories about Spirit Dogs that other dogs had never heard of. Perhaps all dogs had their own Spirit Dogs. Storm's eyes ranged around the Pack until they fell on Arrow, sitting proud and alone as he listened in silence to Alpha's tale.

Do we have our own Spirit Dog, he and I? Storm wondered. *Perhaps there's a Fierce-Dog Spirit that I don't know about. . . .*

Her hackles sprang erect, and she shook off a thrill of suspense.

What does it matter if there is some unknown Fierce-Dog Spirit? This is my Pack! I belong here.

She drew in a breath, and clenched her jaws, feeling the soft night wind ruffle her short fur as if a Wind-Dog had licked her as it passed.

The stories of my Pack: Those are my stories! Their Spirit Dogs are my Spirit Dogs.

They're all I need; they're enough for me.

CHAPTER THREE

"What will we do today, Martha? What will we do?" Storm leaped excitedly around Martha's sturdy legs, nipping at her fur with her baby teeth. "Let's do something fun. I know! You can teach me to swim!"

She was so tiny next to Martha, Storm thought with amazement. Then she realized: she wasn't Storm at all, not yet. . . .

I'm still Lick!

One huge webbed paw swiped her gently, making Storm tumble over on the soft grass, but she wriggled up again, forequarters lowered, tail wagging eagerly. Martha bowled her over once more and Storm lay on her back, squirming with delight as the big dog nuzzled her belly affectionately.

I'm a pup again . . . !

A wave of happiness rippled through her short fur. This was better! This was life when it had been fun, and so much simpler. Hopping to her paws, she panted eagerly as Martha licked her face.

"Where are Wiggle and Grunt? I want to play with them! Where are my litter-brothers?"

Martha gave a soft, gruff laugh, wrinkling her muzzle. "Patience, little one. I'm sure they—"

Then her huge head jerked up, and her dark eyes narrowed. Storm stopped, quivering as she watched her foster-mother snuff the breeze. She pressed close to Martha's flank, feeling the big dog's fur bristle.

Something was wrong. . . .

The clearing that had been so sunny and bright and warm seemed suddenly full of shadows. Darkness shifted at the edge of the trees, and the wind was cold now. A darker shadow slipped between the trunks, or so Storm thought. It was hard to see, hard to think clearly, but there was something out there. Something terrible.

"Martha?" she whispered, her whine trembling. "What is it?"

"Quiet, little one. Wait . . ."

"Is it Blade? Has she come back? Oh Martha, what will we do?" Her whole small body felt cold and vulnerable, and the trees seemed so very big.

Martha turned, dipping her great head to Storm's tiny one. "Oh, Lick," she murmured. "Little dog, I don't know what to do. There's no danger out there."

"But Martha—"

"No danger, little Lick, no darkness in the forest, I promise." Martha's tongue gently caressed her ear. "The darkness is in you."

Cold horror rushed through Storm's body like a freezing river, and the shadows swirled, engulfing her.

And she jerked awake, gasping for breath.

Reeling on her paws, Storm stumbled, then gazed around in a daze, the dream still clinging to her like tendrils of night. Violently she shook herself. Beneath her claws she could feel hard, cold rock, and there were no warm bodies near her, no gentle rise and fall of flanks. She wasn't in the camp; she wasn't with her hunting mates. There was no sound of them, no scent.

The Earth-Dog was still, the night black, but Storm could make out the looming shadows of trees. She became aware, as the dream finally drifted away, that her paw pads hurt, and as she bent to lick them, she realized they were cut and bruised, as if by a long walk over rough ground.

Blinking, Storm forced herself to focus on her surroundings. She knew this place. It was a knoll far from the camp, where Twitch and his friends used to hunt, but still within the new Pack's territory. *How did I get here?*

She had no memory of leaving the camp. She clenched her fangs, shook her head. No, this wasn't her dream any longer. This was real.

Exhausted by panic, she let her head droop as she turned in

the direction of the camp and began to plod back down the rocky slope. *But I don't remember climbing up it.* A fragment of the dream flitted through her brain once more, and she shivered and gave a stifled whimper.

Is this why my paw pads have been hurting lately? Have I done this before?

Panic squeezed Storm's chest. *If I have, how often has it happened?*

The woods seemed darker and deeper than ever, the moon no more than a cold sliver glimpsed now and again between the overhanging branches. The thought of running into a patrol dog horrified her: What would she say? *I don't want to face any questions. How can I give the answers when I don't know them? What if they start thinking I'm odd? That I'm not quite one of them?*

She knew just where Daisy would be on patrol, so she lay quietly in the long weeds until the pale little shape passed, sniffing dutifully at the camp's fringes. Storm held her breath as Daisy paused, raised her head, and sniffed the air as if she'd caught a strange scent. But then she shook her head and moved on, and it was easy enough for Storm to slip through behind her on her belly, staying low and silent.

She thought she was home and safe, thought she had made it back unseen, and her fur began to settle and her breathing to calm. Then she raised her head to see two dark figures cross the path right in front of her.

One halted, turning in shock, and she saw glowing eyes blink in the shadows.

"Storm?" asked the dog. "What are you doing out here?"

"Bella!" The name was hoarse in Storm's throat: *Lucky's litter-sister.* Her heart sank. Beside Bella was the slender, powerful shape of Arrow the Fierce Dog, and he too had cocked his head, eyeing her with suspicious curiosity.

"Yes, Storm." He looked at Bella, then back at her. "What's going on?"

"I . . ." Storm's throat felt dry as dust. *I don't know what's going on, Arrow.* "I couldn't sleep. I thought—I decided to take a walk."

There was a sharp bark of *Liar!* in her own head, but Bella only nodded, and hunched her golden shoulders.

"All right," she murmured. "A walk does help a dog to sleep, it's true. But you ought to get to your den now, Storm. You'll have another hard day's hunting tomorrow."

Storm dipped her head. "You're right, Bella. I am tired." She forced her jaws into a friendly panting grin. "Good night. Good night, Arrow."

She padded on, glad to feel the soft grass of the glade under her sore paw pads again. What she'd told Bella was true: Tiredness weighed on the nape of her neck like a stone, and she felt a wave of it wash through her as she trod heavily through the entrance of the hunters' den. Her nest of leaves had never looked so welcoming, yet she wouldn't be in it for long before the Sun-Dog rose.

It was only when she had curled into it, and her eyelids had almost closed, that the vague, nagging question at the back of her skull finally took shape in her mind. But she was right on the verge of sleep, and just as she thought it, she began to tumble over the edge into blissful unconsciousness. . . .

What were Bella and Arrow doing out there?

CHAPTER FOUR

Storm was surprised at how fresh and awake she felt as she bounded through the woods with the hunting party the next day. It was good to stretch her muscles properly, to feel the tiredness of the previous night fall away with the touch of the cool breeze in her fur.

I won't think about that dream. I won't think about waking up on cold rock, far from my den. That was in the past; now she was hunting in a team led by Lucky, and she was determined to make a good showing for him. The air was cool and crisp and sunlight dappled the forest floor, betraying the scuttle and rush of small prey. It was going to be a *good* day.

The weasel in front of her was fast, but she was faster. Her paws pounded through drifted leaves as she raced to intercept the flash of red fur. It was panicking, darting this way and that in search of escape, but she was too experienced to let it slip away. Lucky was driving it toward her, with Bruno and Breeze, and Bella was out at her flank in case it shot away in a sudden diversion; all she had to do was wait for the weasel to come within reach of her jaws. She could trust Lucky, she thought as she halted and crouched behind a grass tussock.

There was her Beta now, muscles stretching under his golden fur as he raced after the prey. Storm forced herself to stay still and low in the shadow of her tussock; she didn't need to use up all her energy by pouncing for her prey. She could wait for it to come to her. It was as good as dead.

And then Lucky's head jerked abruptly up, his nostrils flaring to scent the air. As his pawsteps faltered, the weasel took its chance. It shot to the side, not yet near enough to Storm's snapping jaws, and darted into the trees. With a flicker of red fur, it was gone.

Breeze skidded to a halt, raising her head to give a howl of frustration and anger. Storm rose to all fours, disbelieving. *He let it get away! It's just like the hunt with Whisper and Arrow! But this is Lucky. . . .*

Does he *hate hunting with me?* The notion crawled inside her skull like a biting insect, making her nape prickle with horror. *Lucky hesitated. He didn't drive the weasel to me. Doesn't he trust me?*

She almost didn't dare look at her Beta, but when she did, Lucky wasn't watching her. He seemed to be paying her no attention at all; he was turning, searching the landscape as if he was hunting for something besides a weasel. And none of the other dogs wore hostile expressions; they all looked just as confused as Storm felt.

Bella gave a yip of bemusement. "Beta, what's going on?"

"Hush, Bella." Lucky's eyes narrowed as he scanned the trees. "Don't you smell it?"

The other dogs glanced at one another, then Bella shrugged and began to sniff at the shifting breeze. Bruno and Breeze tipped their heads back and joined in. There *was* something, thought Storm as a tang of something rich and dark tickled her nostrils.

"Deer?" Bruno echoed her suspicions aloud.

"Not very fresh deer-scent," said Breeze, with a thoughtful wrinkle of her muzzle.

"It's probably long gone," sighed Bella.

All the same, Storm found herself licking her chops. It had been a long time since any of the Pack had tasted the warm flavor of deer, had filled their bellies as only a deer could fill them. But she would wait for Lucky's word. He was their hunt-leader.

"It could be worth tracking," said Lucky at last, slowly. "The scent's faded, but it isn't that old. This deer can't have gone far, and if we brought back a whole carcass it would feed the entire Pack."

Storm bounded to his side. "It's worth a try, Beta."

The other dogs nodded, and at a yelp from Lucky they sprang into the chase, following the scent with their heads low to the ground. The hills rose from here in a series of broad shallow steps away from the Endless Lake. It was hard running, but each dog was fired by a new hunger, and Storm's paws raced in strong, eager strides.

The scent trail grew more pungent as they ran, leading them in a more or less straight line up the slope until it rose abruptly into a black rocky cliff. Storm's pawsteps faltered as she took in the impossible precipice, but only for an instant. In that moment she caught another scent, the tang of a second deer crossing the trail of the first. She was about to bark her discovery to the others when Breeze gave a high yelp.

"Another deer! Over here!"

Storm jerked her head around, surprised. Breeze was some rabbit-chases away, but she was indeed sniffing hungrily at clumps of grass at the foot of the cliff. Bruno bounded toward her, but almost immediately slithered to a stop, plunging his muzzle into the scrubby undergrowth.

"Another!" he barked.

In the next few moments all the dogs were barking, leaping off in different directions, almost bumping into each other in their desperation to follow each new scent. *So many deer!* Storm realized. *A whole Pack of them!*

"Spread out!" barked Lucky commandingly. "Stay calm. Search for the strongest trail and we'll follow that."

"But Beta, none of the scents are fresh," yelped Storm. The words tasted bitter in her mouth, but she knew it was true. However many deer there had been here, they were long gone. The hunting party's chase had been for nothing.

One by one the dogs circled, slower now as the trails faded away, then trotted back till they were clustered in the shadow of the overhanging rock. Bruno scraped at the stony earth with his claws, frustrated, and the others pinned their ears back and shared disappointed growls.

"Maybe this is the place where the deer live," suggested Bella, flicking back one ear. "Maybe this is their camp, and they're away just now, hunting for grass and leaves."

"A camp like ours?" Bruno furrowed the skin above his eyes in puzzlement. "You mean, the deer live in Packs like we do?"

"I don't know," said Bella. "But maybe they do. Maybe there are deer Packs just as there are dog Packs."

"Surely we'd know by now if that was true?" Lucky sounded unsure, and Storm glanced at him in surprise. "I suppose I've seen them in small groups sometimes. But mostly deer just seem to wander in ones and twos."

"Well, a lot of them have been wandering here," sniffed Breeze. She licked her chops longingly.

Storm drew away from their small group to nose at the ground again and scan the hillside. *Packs of deer: What a strange idea.*

And yet she couldn't help thinking again of Alpha's stories. She turned and yipped to the others.

"Maybe this place has something to do with the Golden Deer herself," she suggested. "Perhaps her shadows gather here." She licked her jaws hesitantly. "Don't you feel the breeze? It sweeps across the cliff face. This hillside feels like it could be sacred to the Wind-Dogs."

"Nonsense." Bella flicked her tail dismissively and sat on her haunches. "That's just a pup-tale. Alpha's Mother-Dog invented those stories."

"No." Lucky took a few paces forward, and Storm noticed that the fur on his neck was on end. He pricked an ear, and glanced at the rock face, then away toward the rolling fall of the slope. "The other Spirit Dogs are real; why wouldn't the Wind-Dogs be just as real?"

Bella barked a laugh. "Yes, yes. Of course the Wind-Dogs are as real as the other Spirit Dogs. They're *exactly* as real. All those stories were made up by Mother-Dogs, just to send their pups to sleep. They're no more true than the Fear-Dog, and we know Terror made *him* up out of cobwebs and air."

Storm's jaw felt loose. Her ears drooped, and her tail clamped tight against her rump as she stared at Bella. "You don't think the Spirit Dogs are real? But Martha and Lucky taught me—"

"He's real!" The bark came from Breeze, who stepped forward with an air of angry certainty. "The Fear-Dog is no *story*! He's the fiercest and most powerful of the Spirit Dogs, just as Terror said!"

Storm backed off a pace, then another. Her tail felt as if it was going to disappear between her hindquarters. *The River-Dog is real, and the Forest-Dog and the Sky-Dogs and Lightning . . . all the Spirit Dogs are there, watching over us.* She swallowed hard. *But not the Fear-Dog. He's not real. Lucky said so. I don't want to believe in the Fear-Dog.*

Bella was staring at Breeze with a dumbfounded expression; Breeze looked resentfully defiant. It was Bruno who broke the awkward silence.

"My Alpha believes in the Wind-Dogs," he growled. "And she believes in the Golden Deer. That's good enough for me. It should be good enough for any dog in the Pack."

Every dog watched him, tails tapping the ground thoughtfully.

"I hope," Bruno went on, "that any deer we see today are real ones, not shadows. But whatever prey we find, it has to be real. I don't care if it's not a deer. We must find some food for the Pack, even if it's small. So, do we plan to hunt today? Because this might be where some deer Pack lives, it might indeed. But they're not here *now*."

"Bruno's right," said Lucky after a short, impressed silence. "It's getting late. We need to find something to take back to the Pack."

He turned and trotted back down the slope with his easy, loping grace, but he looked, Storm couldn't help thinking, quite regretful. Bounding to catch up with him, she nudged Lucky's shoulder gently with her muzzle.

"What do you really think that place was?"

He shook his head. "Honestly, Storm? I have no idea. It doesn't matter; we have to find living prey." He gave a growl of gruff amusement. "Creatures that aren't made of air and cobwebs!"

Still unsettled, Storm glanced back over her shoulder at the grassy dip beneath the cliff. It was such a strange place, with its network of scents and its silence, the still absence of any prey. A breeze blew from it to ripple through her fur even as she ran, and she felt a chill in her bones.

Was that the Wind-Dogs? Did they speak to me?

Bella's words had riled her, but now they didn't seem to matter because they rang so hollow. Storm could feel her heart thudding in her rib cage. Of course there were Spirit Dogs, of course there were!

Something rustled in the undergrowth to her side, and Storm almost tripped over her own paws as she was brought back to reality and the present. Bella was looking at her, eyes eager and ears pricked, and Storm nodded meaningfully at her.

There's prey down here!

Bruno was right, she thought as she doubled sideways and sped toward the tangle of brush. Questions were unimportant right now, and so were wild notions about the Spirit Dogs leaping down to earth.

With a rippling shake of her muscles, Storm flung herself into the chase.

CHAPTER FIVE

Today's catch had been poor, Storm thought, ashamed—partly because of their pointless chase after the deer. She dipped her head as they all trailed into the camp later that day, avoiding the gaze of the rest of the Pack. A scrawny squirrel dangled from her jaws, but she wasn't proud of it—*we could have done so much better,* she thought. Breeze carried another squirrel, and Lucky had a rabbit in his mouth—a fairly fat one, but still.

If only we could have found one of those phantom deer . . .

Alpha stretched, rose to her paws and paced forward to greet them and examine their catch. There was concern in her dark eyes as she glanced at Storm, then turned to Lucky.

"Snap's still out with her hunting patrol," she told her Beta. "I'm sure she'll bring something back, and together with your prey, well . . ."

Their Alpha was trying to look on the bright side, Storm knew, but she shouldn't have had to.

"I'm sorry, Sweet," Lucky told her in a low growl. "We should have done better. The Moon-Dog is full tonight, and it's good to have a satisfied belly for the Great Howl." He nuzzled Alpha's flank apologetically.

Storm didn't hear Alpha's reply; as the graceful swift-dog pressed her slender nose to Lucky's ear, Storm turned quickly and trotted away, embarrassed to witness her leaders' easy intimacy.

"Thorn," she barked softly, relieved to spot Fiery and Moon's female pup chatting with the feisty little dog from the former Leashed Pack. "Daisy!"

The two cocked their heads toward her, whining greetings. "Was there no prey out there, Storm?" asked Daisy, letting her tongue loll. "Your catch doesn't seem so good this evening."

Storm lowered her ears, ashamed. "It was pretty scarce, and what there was—well, it was as skinny as we are. But it wasn't that. I'm afraid we got distracted by deer scents."

"Deer?" Thorn's ears pricked enthusiastically.

"Yes, but we couldn't find them," sighed Storm. "We wasted a lot of time. I'm sorry."

It was at the edge of her muzzle to mention the strangeness of the place, and her suspicions about a connection with the Golden Deer, but Daisy was wagging her tail excitedly, and Storm decided it was best to keep her jaws shut.

"Lots of deer scents?" barked the little dog. "Well, maybe if you go back you *will* catch a deer!"

"You were just unlucky," agreed Thorn. "Next time you go to that spot, you'll probably see one!"

"Or *lots*." Daisy licked her chops longingly. "Lots of deer . . ." Her voice faded to a hungry growl.

Storm opened her mouth to calm the two dogs' expectations, but she was interrupted by a furious snarling argument from the nearest corner of the clearing. Turning in surprise, she saw that Rake and Ruff—two patrol dogs who had once been in Twitch's Pack—were facing down Moon. They barked angrily at the farm dog, their muzzles almost touching hers. The fur of all three dogs was raised along their spines. Around them, looking distinctly unsettled, stood Twitch, Thorn's litter-brother Beetle, and a couple of hunters who'd once followed Twitch. Breeze was one of them.

Moon's looking a bit outnumbered, thought Storm anxiously, as Thorn trotted forward, growling, to stand at her litter-brother's side.

"You're not my Alpha dog, Moon!" snarled Rake.

Storm padded up to the knot of hostile dogs, Daisy at her flank. "What's going on? Can't you dogs just listen to Alpha and Beta and get along with each other?"

"We don't want to make trouble," growled Ruff, "but we won't let ourselves be ordered around by just *any* dog." She bared her fangs, and Moon gave her a warning snarl in response.

Wildly, Storm glanced around, and was relieved to see Sweet and Lucky pacing across the clearing toward them. But Rake, Ruff and Moon were still too busy glaring at one another to take any notice. Rake lunged suddenly, his jaws snapping on Moon's fur as she jerked back. She spun and bit savagely at his shoulder as Beetle and Ruff circled, snarling and darting bites at one another.

"I don't take commands from you!" barked Rake again as he dodged Moon's angry jaws. "Alpha said Twitch was in charge of the patrol dogs. That's who tells me what to do—Twitch! Not you!"

Moon stiffened, jaws dripping and blue eyes glittering as the dogs resumed their angry standoff. "You're on guard duty tonight whether you like it or not. Do as you're told."

"Twitch!" Rake spun to face his old Pack leader. "You tell her. She's undermining your authority!"

Twitch didn't seem to want to be involved; in fact, he looked as if he'd rather be anywhere else. Shifting his hindquarters, he glanced from Rake to Moon to Ruff. He gave an uncertain growl, low in his throat, but before he could come up with an answer, Daisy bounded forward.

"You should respect Moon!" she told them in her high-pitched yelp. "We all should!"

Beside her, Thorn and Beetle growled their hearty agreement, then slunk protectively to their Mother-Dog's sides. Storm realized Thorn was on the point of flinging herself violently at Rake's throat. With some desperation, Storm glanced over her shoulder to find Lucky, but he had paused a few paces from the fight. His face was filled with uncertainty.

It was Alpha who shouldered her way into the middle of the quarreling dogs. She stood firm between Thorn and Rake, glaring at them sternly.

Alpha said nothing, but Thorn and Rake both dipped their heads, cowed. Each took a pace backward, as the swift-dog turned on her slim legs, meeting the eyes of the patrol dogs.

"I won't have this," she growled. "Do you hear? The last thing this Pack needs is fighting dogs."

Rake opened his jaws, then seemed to think better of it. He

shut them again, and licked his chops nervously.

"Moon and Twitch are two of the most experienced dogs in this Pack," Alpha went on, with a distinct undercurrent of threat in her soft voice. "They both deserve respect. If I hear of any patrol dog failing to give it to them—to *either of them*—there will be consequences. Serious consequences, do you all understand?"

Every patrol dog lowered his or her eyes, and tails dropped to clamp against their rumps.

"Yes, Alpha," muttered Rake, and Ruff gave a hasty nod of agreement.

"Of course," grunted Thorn.

They kept their gazes down while their Alpha studied them severely, but as she turned dismissively and stalked away, Storm didn't take her eyes off the patrol dogs. From the looks they were giving one another, they weren't at all submissive now. Fangs were subtly bared, eyes flashed with hostility, and as soon as Alpha was out of earshot, there was a distinct low snarling in several throats. Violence was on the edge of breaking out again; Storm could sense it in the air. Even Twitch and Moon, who had always got along so well, were avoiding each other's eyes.

Alpha, with Lucky at her flank, returned to her sleeping-place and flopped carefully down, head on her paws as she watched the patrol dogs from a distance. The tight group was breaking up now, but Storm did not like the way it was dividing. There was a very obvious split as the dogs turned their backs on each other: Twitch's old followers, and the patrol dogs who had originally been with Sweet's Pack. And there were no amicable licks or forgiving nudges as the two groups hurried to opposite sides of the clearing.

Daisy and Thorn were crouching in a huddle with Moon and her other patrollers, but as Storm trotted to join them, Daisy glanced up at her, brown eyes apologetic.

"Storm, if you don't mind . . . I think this is patrol-dog business? We all need to talk. For a bit. Alone?"

Storm hesitated, one paw off the ground. Feeling horribly awkward, she glanced around the camp. The hunt-dogs were all in little groups of their own by now, chatting lazily about their day, and Storm didn't think there was a single cluster of dogs she could butt her way into uninvited. She swallowed as she nodded at Daisy and slunk away from the patrol dogs.

With a suddenness that took her breath away, she was swamped by longing for Martha. In that moment she missed her foster-mother so badly, she wanted to howl to the sky all alone. When Martha had been alive, there had always been at least one dog who was happy to welcome her, to let Storm cuddle against her huge flank and confide her hopes and worries and miseries.

A small shiver ran along Storm's spine as she remembered her dream from the previous night: Martha's kind eyes filling her vision; her warm, gruff voice that had always been full of comfort.

The darkness is in you. . . .

Storm shivered and gave a plaintive whimper. *What's wrong with me?*

Maybe nothing. After all, Lucky had had terrible dreams, once. He'd dreamed of the Storm of Dogs, and the nightmares had tormented him for many journeys of the Moon-Dog. But those dreams had predicted Storm's victory over Blade; they'd been a *good* omen. That wasn't what her dream had felt like. It seemed to promise only horror and darkness.

Storm sat on her haunches, torn by different urges. She licked her jaws and gave a low unhappy whine. In the center of the glade, Lucky lay curled up with Sweet, talking quietly; Storm didn't feel she could interrupt their moment of private intimacy. *But I need to ask someone about my dream, someone who knows what it's like. . . .*

As she hesitated, the undergrowth rustled, and with a crunching of leaves and a snapping of twigs the dogs of the second hunting party trotted into the clearing. Storm breathed a sigh of relief as she got to her paws, tongue lolling. Snap and her hunters had brought a good deal more prey than she, Lucky, and the others had managed. The Great Howl wouldn't be a gloomy affair after all.

Wagging her tail, Storm waited until Alpha had risen to greet the hunters and admire their catch, then took her opportunity. She padded close to Lucky and settled down at his side.

"Storm." He licked her ear affectionately.

"Lucky, can I ask you something?"

"Of course you can." He seemed distracted, preoccupied with Alpha and the hunters, but Storm took a deep breath and plunged on.

"Do you still dream about the Storm of Dogs?"

His sidelong glance was a little startled, but then he shook his golden head and looked back at Snap and Alpha. "No, Storm, that's all over. I haven't dreamed about it since it happened."

"Well." She licked her jaws with a tongue that felt dry. "The thing is, Lucky . . . I had a dream last night. A bad dream."

"Oh, you don't have to worry. All dogs have bad dreams sometimes. It's natural." He nodded toward Snap. "Look at that fine rabbit Snap caught!"

Storm opened her jaws. *But Lucky*, she wanted to blurt out.

Martha said something terrible, and I woke up outside the camp, and I still don't know how I got there, and—

It was no use; she couldn't bring herself to say it. The words dream-Martha had said, Storm realized, were something she was too ashamed to share with any other dog.

Even with Lucky . . .

Because what if it wasn't an ordinary dream? What if, like Lucky's nightmare, it had meant something?

Lucky's dreams, after all, had warned him about a great battle. They hadn't warned him about *himself*!

But what if my dream is true, too?

CHAPTER SIX

Above their heads the Moon-Dog was full and silver, glowing with a light that cast deep shadows. Gazing up at her, Storm's heart felt full, and for a moment all her fears and worries about the dream fell away, as if she'd shaken water from her fur. The Great Howl was the one thing that could always draw the Pack together, make every dog set aside the petty differences and small irritations of the day; it could even make a dog forget the awfulness of a dream—if only for a little while.

I'm counting on it.

The Pack sat, crouched, or sprawled in the center of the clearing, forming a loose circle around Alpha, who gazed transfixed at the night sky. As the mutters of conversations faded, and the Moon-Dog rose higher, the swift-dog tipped back her slender head and parted her jaws. Closing her eyes, she let a howl rise in her throat, swelling until it echoed and resounded in the trees.

One by one, the other dogs joined their voices to Alpha's. The sound grew, the dogs matching their voices together until the howl seemed like a solid, living thing that rippled across their fur and thrilled in their muscles and blood.

Storm's own howl was building inside her, and she raised her jaws to release it. Her cry merged seamlessly with the others, and she felt the stirring joy of the Pack's togetherness.

She paused. *Except we're not all together. . . .*

The sensation of the howl felt thinner than usual; it didn't fill her bones as it should. Sneaking a glance to her side, Storm saw that her suspicions were right. Some of the Pack members weren't howling at all.

Ruff, she realized, catching sight of the female patrol dog's sullen, silent expression. *And Chase. And Breeze . . .*

All dogs of Twitch's old Pack. Are they still angry about that confrontation with Moon? Shocked, Storm lowered her head, her voice catching and halting in her throat.

How can they resist the pull of the Howl? Bewildered, she cocked her ear. Her tail was tight between her hindquarters.

I don't want to be unhappy, not tonight! With a stirring resentment toward the silent dogs, Storm threw her head back once more and rejoined the Howl, giving her voice even more intensity to make up for the surly absentees. Deliberately she shut Ruff and Chase and Breeze out of her mind, forcing herself to focus only on the voices of the Packmates who howled with her. Slowly, inexorably, she felt herself drawn in again, until she was one with her Pack once more, their voices and dog-spirits blending with the night air and rising to the Moon-Dog.

I feel them, she thought with a thrill. *Not my Pack, the Others. The Spirit Dogs. I feel them!*

Beneath her paw pads she could feel the pulse of the Earth-Dog's great heart, beating through the landscape. From far away she heard the rush of the River-Dog, could feel her flow as clearly as she felt the blood in her body. In the trees around her, she was aware of rippling movement in the shadows, and she knew it was the cunning Forest-Dog, who guarded and protected them all. He ran and dodged and hunted there, bringing prey and good luck to the Pack. In her mind's eye she saw the dark glow of his gaze, watching over them.

The Forest-Dog reminds me of Lucky, she thought in a daze of contentment. *But then, he is Lucky's Spirit Dog.*

Who is my *Spirit Dog?* Storm blinked her eyes open to let the brilliant moonlight dazzle her. *Who will guide me, Moon-Dog?*

For a moment she thought the great silver Spirit Dog was really going to answer her. Something filled her head, something huge and wondrous, so that she felt she was floating as she howled.

Then it happened. A darkness blotted out the Moon-Dog's form: the dark running shape of a vast and terrifying Fierce Dog. Cold gripped Storm's heart as her voice caught in her throat again, choking off her howl.

As it moved across the Moon-Dog's form, the dark Spirit Dog seemed to pause, turn, and fix eyes on Storm that were darker than the night sky, but which glittered with a starlike glow.

A Sky-Dog! Yet even as she thought that, Storm knew it was no Sky-Dog. This was a Spirit Dog she had never seen before, one she had never even heard of. His terrible eyes remained locked on hers for a moment longer; then he was turning, and his long loping stride carried him away across the blackness of the sky. The Moon-Dog's light glowed fiercely on the Pack once more.

The other dogs were still singing their cries, but Storm's body felt empty of breath. She couldn't give voice to a whimper, much less a howl. Glancing to one side and the other, she realized none of the others had even paused in their song. The eyes of her Pack-mates were closed in ecstasy, or they were riveted on the light of the Moon-Dog. Storm realized the truth like a bite to her belly.

No other dog saw what I saw!

In desperation she scanned the upturned faces of her Pack-mates. *Did no dog see the fierce Spirit Dog? Did I imagine him?*

No! She realized that, with absolute certainty, when her eyes locked with Arrow's.

The other Fierce Dog was not howling, either. He was watching Storm, his dark eyes knowing, as if they shared a secret. A great and terrible *family* secret . . .

The shock of connection made Storm jerk her head away, and she stared up at the sky in near panic. *I am not like Arrow! I am not the same as him!*

She was one of this Pack! She'd been raised by Lucky and Martha, not by Blade; she'd learned to be a true, kind, and loyal friend, not a bloodthirsty warrior-dog. *I'm not like Arrow! I was never one of Blade's Pack!*

No matter how hard she tried, though, she could not raise her voice again to join with the Pack's howling. And she realized, with a shock, that it was because of fear. *I don't want to see that Spirit Dog again. If I raise my head and howl, he might return.*

I don't want him to come back. . . .

Feeling shrunken back to pup-size, she sat quietly, tail between her legs, deliberately avoiding Arrow's gaze. He was still looking at her, she knew it, but she would not meet those conspiratorial eyes again.

As the Great Howl faded, Storm sat silently, staring straight ahead. Only when most of her Packmates had risen and shaken themselves and headed for their sleeping dens with contented barks and growls of good night did she finally get to her paws.

I'm not going to talk to Arrow about this. I don't care what he thinks.

Breeze, though, was glancing up at the Moon-Dog as she paced toward her den, and Storm licked her chops, filled with curiosity. *Why didn't Breeze join the Howl? She was so loyal to the Spirit Dogs earlier, when she argued with Bella; she believes in the Spirits and trusts them. Even if she was angry, why wouldn't Breeze howl?*

Determinedly, Storm caught up to pad at her flank. "Breeze, why didn't you join in the Howl?" she blurted out. "You and your friends? Don't you want to feel part of the Pack?"

Breeze shot her a thoughtful look as she licked her jaws. "I can't speak for the others," she said at last. "Maybe they were just too angry to howl tonight."

"But that's just what the Great Howl does," pointed out Storm. "It soothes anger, brings us all together! And the Spirit Dogs—"

"I know that's the idea, that it unites the Pack," admitted Breeze, hesitating to sniff the night air, "and I trust in the Spirit

Dogs. But for me, it wasn't the anger. Maybe for Ruff and Rake and Chase, but not me. I've never howled with the Pack."

"What?" Storm pricked her ears, shocked.

"It's true. When we were Terror's Pack, we never howled. We didn't want to attract the attention of the Fear-Dog."

"That's ridiculous," exploded Storm.

"Is it?" Breeze hunched her shoulders against a shudder. "Think what you like, but Terror knew about these things. When Twitch took over as our Alpha he reinstated the Howl, but I never joined in, even then." Furtively she peered into the shadows around the glade, then nudged her head closer to Storm, and whispered nervously, "I don't want the Fear-Dog to find me. The way he found Terror . . ."

Storm stared after Breeze as the hunt-dog hurried to her den. *What a ridiculous notion. Terror put the fear of . . . well, the fear of the Fear-Dog into that Pack.*

It's not true. Lucky said there was no such thing as a Fear-Dog. And there isn't.

All the same, Storm shivered as she crept to her own nest of soft leaves and grass, and she raked her bedding with her claws to enclose her body more snugly. Even then, she couldn't get comfortable. The chill was in her bones, not in the night air, and her snug nest felt as if it was full of stones. She shifted restlessly, twisting and turning.

Was it the Fear-Dog I saw?

The thought popped unwelcome into Storm's skull, making her snap her head up and pant for breath. Lucky had said the Fear-Dog was a figment of Terror's warped imagination—but Lucky had been wrong before. . . .

Arrow had seen that Spirit Dog too. Could he and Storm have brought the Fear-Dog down on the Pack?

Squeezing her eyelids tight shut, she forced herself to think only of drifting into unconsciousness. *I will go to sleep, I will . . .*

Except that I can't. Her legs kicked in frustration. *I'll never sleep again. . . .*

What? What's going on?

Storm's legs were not thrashing against leaves and grass anymore; they were bounding freely over the forest floor. Urgency seized her chest, and she picked up speed.

There was something she had to do. She had to get there now. She had to do this!

Even though she couldn't remember exactly what the vital thing was . . .

The shadow that raced at her side did not belong to her. She could hear its footfalls, and she could make out its darkness from the corner of her eye, but she didn't want to look. Instead she ran faster than ever.

"You can't outrun me," said a voice. "You never could. I will always be with you."

This time, Storm made herself look. She turned her head to glare at the darkness.

"Blade!" She wasn't out of breath, yet she couldn't seem to run fast enough to outpace the shadowy Fierce Dog. "You're dead, Blade. You can't be here."

Blade peeled back her lips in a scornful snarl. "You think it's that easy to get rid of me? I'm stronger than death, Storm. I know the truth about you; I've always known it. That's why I'll always be at your side. That's why I'll always be with you."

Storm licked her jaws, but she couldn't make them moist. Her tongue was coated in dust and ashes. "Are you the Fear-Dog?"

Blade barked a hollow laugh. "You know better than that, Storm."

Storm couldn't look away. She could only run, and stare in horror at Blade, and try not to fall.

"The Fear-Dog is patrolling tonight." Blade's whispering voice was dark and deadly. "But I am not the dog who brought him here."

Storm skidded, stumbled to a halt, crashed to the ground. Leaves and grass broke her fall, but there were sharp stones beneath them, and she yelped in pain and terror.

* * *

And woke up. She froze in disbelief. She hadn't fallen at all; she was on her four paws, in a turmoil of leaves and sand where she must have skidded and twisted. Her flanks heaved as she fought to control her desperate breathing.

Storm eyed the darkness around her. Spun on her haunches, and stared.

She was no longer in the camp. She was no longer in the glade. She was deep in the forest. And for the second time, she had no memory of how she had gotten there.

CHAPTER SEVEN

Light and sound finally penetrated Storm's restless sleep. Blinking painfully, she curled into a tighter ball, trying to sink back into unawareness, but it was useless. A damp nose nudged her flank and a friendly voice teased her.

"Are you ever going to get up, young Storm?"

She kept her eyes shut tight. The affectionate growl was Mickey's, but she couldn't face even the kind Farm Dog. Focusing on making the rise and fall of her flanks regular and slow, she heard his gruff, fond laughter.

"Lazy pup, I know you're not asleep." He nuzzled her. "All right, stay there for a bit."

I really need to, she thought guiltily. *It's tiring going for walks in the night. Walks I don't even remember . . .*

It was impossible to go back to sleep now, though. Through

the underbrush she could hear the low voices of dogs arguing. Again! What was it now?

Probably the same thing, she realized with a heavy sigh. The voices belonged to, among others, Thorn and Breeze, so no doubt it was another quarrel about the patrol dogs failing to respect Moon's orders.

It all seemed so very ordinary, so everyday compared to last night. Her frantic dash-and-stumble back to camp in the darkness was like a vague and distant memory now; she could even convince herself it hadn't been real. Except that she remembered vividly the terror she'd felt, running blindly, convinced that the Fear-Dog was stalking her, that at any moment she'd feel his red claws in her hide. She'd have sworn she could hear the echoing thud of his paws on the earth as he hunted her down.

It had been easy enough to sneak past Daisy and Dart, who had been on night patrol, but she couldn't help the bite of worry in her gut. If this was going to happen again, she couldn't rely on every dog being unwary. Sooner or later one of the Pack would catch her as she tried to creep back into the camp. What if the dreams never left her in peace?

It's not something I want to have to explain to any dog.

There were other voices around her; she could hear them

clearly with her eyes shut. Lucky and Alpha were murmuring to each other. It was a much more friendly, reassuring sound than the argument. She felt safer with her Alpha and her Beta watching over the Pack—at least while the Sun-Dog shone overhead.

Night could be a different nest of rats. But I can't worry about that just now.

"My Mother-Dog used to tell me stories of the Spirit Dogs," Lucky was telling Alpha, his rumbling voice fond. "Stories about Lightning, and the Forest-Dog, and the Sky-Dogs. Did your Mother-Dog tell you about the Wind-Dogs?"

"She did, Lucky." Storm heard Alpha's small grunt as she rolled over in the grass and wriggled into a more comfortable position. "She told us a Wind-Dog story every night."

"And what stories will you tell our pups, Sweet?" There was lazy amusement in Lucky's voice.

"I'll tell them about all the Spirit Dogs, yours and mine." Alpha laughed. "And so will you, I expect."

Storm felt a pang of envy. Her own Mother-Dog had never had the chance to tell her any stories.

"I'll tell you one of my Mother-Dog's stories, shall I?" murmured Alpha.

"Go on." Lucky sounded more alert. Storm could visualize his ears pricking up, the light of interest sparking in his brown eyes.

"All right." Alpha sighed contentedly. "Long ago, Lucky, at the time of the First Dogs, it's said that the Sun-Dog never slept at all."

"What, never?" Lucky had made his voice as innocent as a pup's, and Alpha huffed a laugh.

"Never. The Sun-Dog was too possessive of the sky, you see. He liked to run and play and bask in that great blue field all the time. The Sky-Dogs tried to persuade him to rest, and to give the Moon-Dog a chance to run and hunt, but he wouldn't listen. He ordered the Sky-Dogs to go away, because he had more power than they did, and he said he would never yield his place to the Moon-Dog."

"Bossy old Sun-Dog," growled Lucky, a grin in his gruff voice. "But I expect the First Dogs liked being able to hunt all day."

"Oh, no, they did not! The First Dogs were always tired, because they couldn't sleep in the light of the Sun-Dog. And the Moon-Dog felt sorry for them. She has always looked after dogs, and given them peace to howl and love and rest and sleep, so that they needn't always be hunting.

"So she set off to speak to the Wind-Dogs. She knew they too loved dogs. Ever since Earth-Dog was born and the world came to be, the Wind-Dogs have loved to play with dogs, chasing and racing them, and the dogs have loved the Wind-Dogs back. And the Wind-Dogs, of course, loved the swift-dogs best of all. Because only swift-dogs could really keep up with them."

"Hmph," grunted Lucky, but he gave a sigh of contentment.

"So the Moon-Dog asked the Wind-Dogs to chase away the Sun-Dog, and after a long struggle, they did. Now Moon-Dog could look over the world eternally, and the First Dogs could have peace and rest."

"Well, that was good, then." Lucky was back in his mock pup-voice.

"It certainly wasn't, young dog!" Alpha was really playing up the role of Mother-Dog, thought Storm sleepily. "The First Dogs could never hunt, you see, and they grew hungry! They slept all the time, but were never warm, because the sky was forever cold.

"So the Sun-Dog and the Moon-Dog and the Wind-Dogs at last came together to make a pact. The Wind-Dogs agreed to let Sun-Dog run for half the day, so long as he went to his rest and let the Moon-Dog take the other half. So from that day on, Sun-Dog and Moon-Dog shared the sky, and the true lives of dogs could begin—hunting in the daytime, and resting in the night."

As the two older dogs fell quiet again, Storm found she was drowsy after all. Listening to her Alpha, she had felt like a pup again. But she would have had better questions than Lucky. . . .

Why would the powerful Sun-Dog run from the Wind-Dogs, Alpha? The strongest dog is always the one who gives orders. That's how it should be. . . .

She had almost drifted back into a doze when violent barking shattered her peace and sent her jumping to her paws. She squeezed out of her den and shook off the fuzzy drowsiness. There was no point pretending to sleep anymore.

Her eyes fell on Sunshine as the little Omega scrambled to her paws nearby. The small dog's black button-eyes looked anxious and fearful. Poor Sunshine tried so hard to be a Wild Dog, but her fluffy little body was not as well suited to the wilderness as the other dogs'. Storm gave her a reassuring whine and licked her nose.

"What's going on?" whimpered the Omega. "Why is there more fighting?"

"It's just the patrol dogs squabbling again," Storm told Sunshine with a sigh. She felt more annoyed with them for upsetting Sunshine than for disturbing her own sleep.

"Don't you dare think you can take over," came Thorn's snarling voice. "You left this Pack, Twitch! You went off to find another one, a *mad* Pack. Just because you came back to fight the Fierce Dogs, it doesn't mean you're in charge now."

A dog brushed past Storm's shoulder on his way toward the quarreling dogs, and her ears pricked when she saw it was Lucky. *He'll sort them out*, she thought grimly, and followed him.

"What's going on?" their golden-furred Beta demanded.

Thorn's head snapped around, and her eyes widened. "Beta!" She licked her jaws, then clenched her fangs, and sat on her haunches. Her voice grew stronger and clearer. "I want to make a challenge. I'm challenging Twitch!"

Storm took a breath with shock, looking from Twitch to Thorn. "That's not fair!"

Thorn stepped one aggressive pace toward her. "Why not? It's Pack law!"

Storm looked around at the other dogs. She licked her chops and swallowed. "I know that. And it's true that any dog can challenge another, anytime—but Thorn, you're young and fast. I've practice-fought you often, and I know you're strong." Storm took a nervous breath, knowing every eye was on her. She wished some dog would speak up in support of her, but there was only silence. "How can Twitch possibly fight you, Thorn?"

Twitch, after all, had only three legs, and he wasn't a true fighter. He'd become his own Pack's Alpha for his guile and intelligence, not for his strength or fighting ability. *Does Thorn really plan to take his place as head patrol dog?* It didn't seem right to Storm, and she was sure Lucky would agree.

"*I challenge Twitch*," said Thorn again defiantly, ignoring Storm and staring at her Beta.

Lucky glanced uncertainly at Alpha. The swift-dog hesitated for only a moment; then Storm saw her slim head move in a tiny nod.

They're going to let this happen! Storm's jaw loosened with shock.

Lucky took two paces into the center of the glade, and turned to gaze around at the gathering Pack. He placed his two forepaws on a low rocky outcrop. Dogs from every corner of the camp were padding curiously forward, cocking their ears, growling questions to one another.

"Thorn the patrol dog," declared Lucky in a ringing bark, "challenges Twitch the lead patrol dog."

With that he stepped back from his rock, turned, and walked back to join the circle of watching dogs. Alpha paced silently to his side, and nodded to the two challengers.

Slowly Thorn circled Twitch, who eyed her warily as he turned. Already he was off balance, Storm realized. Thorn's tactic of constant motion was clever, disturbing the poise of her three-legged opponent.

"I'm fighting for my Mother-Dog," barked Thorn, pausing in her pacing to glare at Twitch. "I'm fighting for her place—to prove *he* can't steal it."

"Wait," growled Storm, her hackles rising. "Is that allowed? Can Thorn even do that—fight for *Moon* to be top patrol dog?"

Lucky glanced at Alpha, but neither of them responded.

Storm clenched her jaws. *What's going on? Thorn's going to humiliate Twitch for no reason other than pride—hers and her Mother-Dog's!* It seemed so stupid and unnecessary, and Storm laid her ears back with anger.

"Beta!" she barked.

Lucky shook his head slowly. He wasn't even looking at Storm; he was watching Moon, steadily and expectantly.

He thinks Moon's going to put a stop to this. But she won't! And indeed, Moon only stared at her pup and at Twitch, and stayed silent.

"It's all right, Storm." Twitch's husky growl was perfectly calm. "I accept Thorn's challenge."

"Wait!" A low, aggressive bark rang out across the clearing. "If Thorn can fight for Moon, then any other dog can fight for Twitch!"

Storm glanced at Lucky, who was silenced by surprise. Alpha

herself looked startled. They both turned to the dog who had spoken: Breeze.

Storm felt her heart swell in her chest, and her blood race through her muscles. *Of course—Breeze is talking sense! I can beat Thorn for Twitch—and that's as fair as anything about this challenge!* She took three paces forward and raised her head to speak.

"I'll do it." Another dog stepped into the circle before Storm could draw breath to offer. He had a mottled brown-and-cream coat marked by the scars of many battles; he was one of Terror's former Pack.

"Woody?" said Lucky, his tail twitching. He looked, thought Storm, as if he didn't like how things were going.

"Yes. I'll fight for Twitch." The tough hunt-dog swung his head to eye Thorn and Moon. "You have your champion, Moon; now Twitch has his. That makes this a more equal contest. Do you agree, Alpha?"

The swift-dog dipped her head in acknowledgment. "I do agree." She and Lucky shared a resigned sigh.

Storm felt a prickle of guilty pleasure in her fur. Woody was a lot bigger than Thorn, and he had much more fighting experience; she remembered very well how skillfully and fiercely he'd fought in the Storm of Dogs. Thorn, as far as Storm was concerned, deserved a good beating for her unjust challenge. She pricked her ears and watched with a new sense of hope, as Woody clawed the earth aggressively.

Alpha still seemed hesitant; this kind of conflict, Storm knew, was not what the swift-dog would want for her Pack. But Alpha spoke firmly.

"Thorn, you issued the challenge. You may withdraw it if you wish, and without shame, but it is your choice."

Thorn didn't tear her gaze from the burly form of Woody. All she did was stiffen her shoulder muscles and inhale a deep, determined breath.

"No," she said. "I won't withdraw. I'll fight Woody."

Tension hummed in the still air of the clearing as the dogs formed a circle around the two challengers. Storm found she could hardly breathe; Thorn might be of her original Pack, but she very badly wanted Woody to win this fight.

It was Thorn who made the first move, hurling herself at Woody in a full-on charge at his throat, as if she hoped to end the fight before it had really begun. *I taught her that move,* Storm realized, her neck fur bristling with resentment.

Woody, though, was too big and strong to be knocked down

so easily. He shrugged Thorn off, twisting away from her jaws and shunting his body hard into hers while she was still off balance. Thorn thudded to the earth, rolled, and sprang back onto her paws. She attacked again with barely a pause for breath, but Woody was obviously expecting such a rash move from the young dog. He dodged, ducked, and charged with his full weight, crashing into Thorn's exposed belly and sending her tumbling. As she tried to rise, he grazed his teeth harshly along her shoulder, nearly drawing blood. Thorn yelped and slithered sideways, then struggled to her feet. They faced each other, panting and snarling.

It'll be a lesson for her, thought Storm with grim satisfaction. *A painful one, but maybe she needs it. Especially if she's too stupid to back down right now.*

"Stop!" The bark rang out in the charged silence, and every dog turned. Twitch limped forward to the center of the circle, and stood between Thorn and Woody.

"Twitch?" Lucky asked, after a quizzical pause.

"Stop the fight," growled Twitch. He nuzzled Woody's shoulder lightly. "I appreciate the loyalty you've shown, Woody, but my rank in this Pack isn't worth injury to two good dogs." He nodded at Thorn. "Nor is it worth a fight between you. Let Moon be the lead patrol dog. She's welcome to my position, and she'll do a fine job. Let that be the last of this."

He turned, a little awkward on his three legs, and dipped his head respectfully to a surprised Moon. After a moment, she nodded back.

Most of the Pack dogs were speechless, and that, thought Storm, was probably a good thing. She couldn't think of a thing to say herself; she felt as if Woody had butted her in the belly.

Some of Twitch's former Pack, though, were muttering under their breath, growling complaints. Woody looked shocked, as well he might; Breeze and Chase, Ruff, and Rake looked downright sullen. The rest of the Pack shifted uneasily, but no dog raised a voice in objection.

Alpha got to her paws, eyeing all three of the dogs in the circle. She nodded thoughtfully. "I understand why you were Alpha of your Pack, Twitch. You put the Pack above yourself. That's why you earn such loyalty, I think." She touched Woody's shoulder with her long nose, then gave Twitch a friendly lick. "I agree: Moon should be lead patrol dog."

The muttering among Twitch's former Pack grew slightly louder.

"But," she went on, raising her voice. "It's past time for us to create a new rank for Twitch. It's right that his old Pack have such faith and trust in him, and it's not surprising that many of you look to him to guide you. He's a good leader and a fine dog, and his talents would be wasted as a patrol dog." She brushed Twitch's nose with her own. "Twitch, you will be Third Dog in this Pack, ranking only below me and Lucky."

Snap sat down abruptly, out of sheer shock. Her jaw was slack. "But, Alpha. The hunters have always ranked above the patrol dogs in this Pack. And Twitch can't hunt!"

"That's beside the point," the swift-dog told her, her eyes narrowing. "I am the Alpha of this Pack, and I know what makes sense for us here and now. Packs can change, and this is the right thing for us."

Lucky's tail beat the earth approvingly. "It's a perfect solution," he barked.

That, it seemed, was the cue some of the dogs needed to express their own approval. From around the circle dogs spoke up, barking and whining in praise of Alpha's clever idea, congratulating Twitch on his promotion.

"Well done, Twitch!" yelped Daisy.

"You'll make a tremendous third in command," added Bruno gruffly. "Alpha has been wise."

"Yes! Good decision, Alpha," panted Mickey.

Storm hadn't realized how tense her muscles were until she sagged with relief, and her own tail began wagging with enthusiasm. It had been a horrible moment, but Alpha had solved the problem with her usual elegance. Storm let her tongue loll happily as she watched the three leaders pad out of the circle together, quietly discussing Twitch's new duties.

A movement caught Storm's attention, and she glanced sideways. Thorn had moved to stand by Beetle, and she was growling something in his pricked ear. Nothing good, judging by the tightness of her jaws and the angry glare of her brother. And Breeze was still and silent, her gaze fixed on Moon. Moon herself wore a confused and slightly hurt expression, as if she couldn't quite work out what had just happened.

A chill of apprehension rippled down Storm's spine. *I thought Alpha had solved the problem.*

But not for all dogs, she hadn't. Storm had the distinct sense that some were only pretending to accept their Alpha's extraordinary decision.

I've got a horrible feeling this isn't over. . . .

CHAPTER EIGHT

There was coolness between and beneath Storm's paw pads as she paced across the ground. A strange, wet, sticky coolness. She dipped her head, surprised, to look below her.

Not ground at all. The surface she walked on was slick and shifting, a green-sheened dark liquid that was thicker than water. Her paws sank into it a little, but it didn't swallow her up, not if she kept walking.

Only if she stopped did it begin to suck her down. . . .

Hurriedly she picked up her stride. All around her moonlight shimmered on the odd surface, and the Moon-Dog was reflected in a glossy path of bright silver. Storm felt herself drawn to look down again, and in the smooth surface she caught a clear glimpse of her own face.

So angry! She jumped, startled. *Snarling like a wolf . . .*

Shocked, she halted with one paw raised; instantly she began to sink into the shining mass. I'm not angry! *Her face felt calm, her jaws relaxed.* I'm not snarling!

So why would her reflection . . .

"It's your real face. That's why."

Storm whirled, tugging her paws free of the glossy, treacherous liquid, and found herself staring into the eyes of Fang.

Fang, her litter-brother. But he was dead. . . .

Yes. Dead. He must be. There were two deep, red holes in his neck where Blade had sunk in her teeth and stolen his life. No blood ran from the savage puncture marks, though. None would, Storm realized. Because—this was not real.

It wasn't real, but that didn't stop her from giving a yelp of fear at the sight of Fang.

She shifted her paws, trying not to sink further. Fang gazed at her, full of sadness.

"It's your true self you see, Storm. The Earth-Blood never lies."

"No!"

"Yes, Storm. You think you're not as fierce as Blade, not as vicious. But how many dogs could be as brutal as she was?" *He gave her a mournful smile, and the puncture marks in his neck gaped as he shook his head.* "It doesn't mean you don't have savagery in you. Can't you feel the rage inside? It's there, and you know it."

"No. It isn't. I don't!"

"*Really? Each time those dogs of your Pack look at you with fear, every time you feel their unease as you pass too close . . . you grow angry. Don't you, litter-sister? There's darkness within you, and you want to let it out. Why shouldn't you? You want to strike out your claws at those mistrustful dogs, those dogs who have never had faith in you. You want to bite them, kill them, shut them up. You want them to wish they'd never—*"

"NO!" *Struggling to turn, to tear her paws from the sucking Earth-Blood, Storm tried to run. Every step was a battle, a painful dragging agony, and as she laid each paw back on the surface it sank even further. One foreleg plunged deep into the Earth-Blood and would not move. Then the other. She felt the liquid creep slowly up her legs, tickle her neck. She lifted her head, fighting for air.*

It was no use. She was going under the Earth-Blood, and there was nothing she could do to save herself. . . .

Storm woke sharply, on her four paws among starlit tree trunks, blood thudding hard in her ears.

A long sigh escaped her and she closed her eyes. She'd almost stopped feeling surprised when this happened, she realized with a heavy heart. Of course she was far from the camp. Of course she had no memory of coming here. Her head sagged.

Still. It's good to feel solid ground under my paws again, even if I sleepwalked onto it.

Storm gave her coat a thorough shake, then trod a circle,

eyeing the trees to try to get her bearings. When her nostrils flared to snuff the early-morning breeze, she could easily detect the strong scents of her Packmates. They were close by, then; she hadn't wandered too far.

But why does it happen at all? No dog walks while they sleep; it isn't possible!

She was so tired of it, tired of having to creep back to her own camp and avoid the watchful eyes of her own friends. *This is how a dog would approach the camp if it was attacking. This is how invaders would behave. But I'm not an intruder. This is my Pack!*

"And what are you doing sneaking around?" The abrupt bark was full of suspicion.

Storm spun guiltily to face Dart. Licking her jaws, she stilled the trembling of her limbs. *Don't look ashamed*, she told herself crossly. *You have nothing to be ashamed of!*

Nothing except that you're a Strange Dog, an Odd Dog, a Dog Who Walks in Her Sleep . . .

But she couldn't explain any of that to Dart. If she went on wearing this guilty expression, the small brown patrol dog really would think she was up to something.

"Nothing, Dart. I just . . . went for a walk." That was true enough.

Dart extended her forelegs and gave a luxurious stretch and

a yawn. Clearly she hadn't been awake for long. "Were you out hunting by yourself? Because that's not allowed, remember." Dart lashed her jaws with her tongue and yawned again. A light of something mean entered her dark eyes. "There are Pack rules. Beta might think you're something special, but that doesn't mean you can do as you like."

A growl rose in Storm's throat at the unfairness of it, but she bit it back, and shook herself. *Rage. I shouldn't feel such rage! That's what Fang spoke about in my dream.*

"I told you," she snapped, "I just went for a walk. I couldn't sleep. Would you rather I fidgeted all night and woke every dog in the Pack?"

Dart snorted with disdain. "Suit yourself. I'll never understand Fierce Dogs."

This time Storm had to tense every muscle in her forelegs and dig her claws into the earth to stop herself from flying at Dart. She might have barked in fury anyway, if something hadn't distracted her: under her paw pads, the grass was wet and cool with dew.

Like the stuff in my dream. The liquid that sucked me down. Is Earth-Blood nothing but dew? Momentarily bewildered, she hesitated and glanced down, and in that instant Dart turned and sauntered off toward the camp.

Storm gritted her teeth and glared at the patrol dog's disappearing haunches. As Dart left, Bella padded toward Storm, giving Dart a curious glance as she passed.

"Are you all right, Storm?" Bella sat down, tilting her head. She might be inquisitive, thought Storm, but at least she wasn't hostile.

"I'm fine," she managed to mutter. "I haven't been sleeping well, that's all. I went for a walk." *All these half-truths*, she thought remorsefully, *but there's no way I'm telling Bella—or any dog—the real story.*

"Storm, you need to pull yourself together." Bella's growl was kind, though. "There are dogs who are uneasy around you already. Don't give them extra reasons to mistrust you."

"I'm not trying to!" barked Storm, exasperated. "I don't go out of my way to unsettle them, believe me." Her voice lowered to a resentful growl. "I just seem to manage that without any effort."

Bella stood up to give her ear a friendly lick. "Try anyway, won't you? The last thing the Pack needs is to think Fierce Dogs can't be trusted."

Storm pricked her ears in surprise. *What does she mean by that?* The Fierce Dog Pack wasn't a threat anymore; it had fallen apart after Blade's death. And there were only two Fierce Dogs in this Pack: Storm herself, and Arrow.

"There's peace in our Pack now, of course," Bella went on, "but it's fragile. Do you understand, Storm? There are dogs who can't let go of the fear; it clings to their hearts. It wouldn't take much for them to turn on one another." Bella's deep brown eyes were anxious; she seemed desperate to make Storm understand. "You're not a pup anymore. You're a strong dog, you've proven that! You need to start acting like it. A strong, grown-up dog, a full member of the Pack. You don't want our Pack to split, like Earth-Dog in a Growl!"

Storm opened her jaws, unsure how to respond. But before she could say anything, the calm air was shattered by a roaring blast of wind.

She and Bella leaped to their paws, hackles bristling as they scanned the sky through the branches. This was no natural gust, Storm could tell. It wasn't the Wind-Dogs who were making the trees shake. Storm's heart slammed against her rib cage. There were dark shapes in the sky above them.

"Loudbirds!" barked Bella in horror.

Together they dashed back into the camp, as the wind stripped leaves from the trees all around them and branches were torn and tossed in the gale. In the glade dogs were hurtling from one corner to another, or spinning on their haunches, or standing dead still and shivering, and the air was filled with terrified yelps and barks. Sunshine cowered beneath a jutting rock, her tiny white body trembling.

"Run!" barked Bruno.

"Where to?" howled Ruff.

"We have to do something!" That was Woody, but he didn't seem to have any ideas himself. He was dodging from side to side in indecision.

Storm crouched, flattening her ears and tail as she stared up into the sky. The loudbirds were flying low, wings whirring, one directly behind the other; they circled lower and lower before rising again. All the time they made that terrible roaring, and the wind of their wings lashed the forest and the camp. The barking, panicking dogs could barely make themselves heard.

Leaping up, Storm dashed to where Lucky was staring upward, his fur rippling in the storm the loudbirds had created.

"What are they doing?" barked Storm. "Are the loudbirds going to take our camp?"

Lucky didn't answer. He turned to gaze at Alpha, and there was intense worry in his eyes.

Alpha, realized Storm at once. *Is she our most vulnerable dog right now? Can she even run very fast while carrying a litter?*

And if she can't run, what do we do?

"Beta!" yelped Storm, but he still stood, immobile. To her shock, he took no notice of her at all, or of the frantic dogs racing around the glade. He stepped deliberately to Alpha and stood in front of her, paws planted firmly on the earth, glaring up at the loudbirds as if he was acting as a barrier between her and them.

He's not acting like an Alpha or a Beta, realized Storm, her heart plummeting. *He's not concerned for the Pack, and he's not calming them down. He's thinking only of his mate and their unborn pups.*

In that case, some other dog had to do it. Storm spun on her haunches and raced back across the clearing. She almost tripped across the panicking Snap, but shouldered her aside and bounded on, barking.

"Calm down! Every dog, be quiet!"

Rake turned on her, wild-eyed. "But they're coming for us!"

"No, they aren't. Not yet." Storm tipped her head back to give a penetrating howl. "Calm down, all of you!"

The racket in the glade subsided, just a little, as dogs began to halt, panting, and turn to watch Storm. They were desperate for leadership at this instant. That was her only way to get through to them.

"Listen," she barked fiercely, her voice carrying even above the loudbirds' roar. "Loudbirds have no teeth, no claws. They aren't predators! All they're good for is carrying longpaws."

"But if they land in our camp—" whimpered Daisy.

"Yes, they have to land *first*, before they can hurt us. And loudbirds are slow! We'll have plenty of time to escape if they decide to perch here."

Whisper bolted forward, pressing his flank tightly against Storm's; she could feel the terrified tremors in his skin. "But even if we run, where will we go?" he whined. "We'll never find another camp as good as this one! Where will we find prey? Storm, help us!"

Storm clenched her jaws. The last thing she needed right now was Whisper's cowering hero-worship. It riled her even more now that there was such a need for calm and focus from the whole Pack.

Breeze had stopped dead, and she was glaring at Storm. "You really think you should be giving the orders?" she snarled.

Storm stiffened so abruptly, her legs trembled. She wanted to let out a bewildered whine, but she was speechless with shock. Breeze had never spoken like that to her before. *So why—*

"If your leaders are in no shape to make a decision"—Breeze jerked her head at Lucky and Alpha—"then it's *Twitch* we should look to!"

Lucky's head snapped around, and there was shock in his eyes. But if he felt any guilt for his lapse in leadership, it was clearly still overwhelmed by his confusion and his concern for Alpha. He backed even closer to his mate, who was panting with alarm as she licked her swollen flanks.

"Breeze is right! You're not our leader!" Dart's snarl came from behind Storm, and she twisted to face the small dog, but Dart was not alone. Ruff and Rake were eyeing Storm too, lips peeled back from their teeth.

"But," Storm began, confused and hurt. "I don't mean—"

At that moment, to her intense relief, Twitch himself bounded forward on his three legs. "We can all argue about leadership some other time," he barked, a steely look in his eyes. "For now, get yourselves organized. If we have to run, we must be ready. We will all go together."

Storm felt like leaping on him and licking his ears with gratitude, but she only dipped her head. She was about to bark her agreement, too, but above their heads something was changing. The racket of the loudbirds was not as deafening, and the terrible gale of their spinning wings was lessening.

"They're flying back upward," she barked, filled with renewed hope.

"Are they leaving?" Mickey backed a few paces, narrowing his eyes at the sky.

"Yes! They're flying away!" Daisy leaped off the ground with all four paws, she was so relieved and excited.

A few last disturbed leaves whirled down, pattering onto the grass, and the high branches calmed their wild thrashing. Around them the more slender trees creaked back upright, and birds began to sing hesitantly again. The loudbirds circled higher and higher until they were nothing more than faint black dots flying toward the sunup horizon.

The whole forest seemed to shiver and relax. Bruno gave his shaggy coat a violent shake. Ruff licked her black flank, seeming angry at her own panic. Sunshine crept out, trembling, from beneath her rock. All around Storm, dogs were shaking themselves, wagging their tails, and letting out yelps and barks of relief. Storm's own flanks were heaving, and she was panting with exertion.

"Who do you think you are, Storm?" Dart seemed to have recovered quickly, and her bark was vicious.

"She's making a play to be Alpha, if you ask me," snarled Ruff.

"Packmates." Lucky bounded forward before Storm could even open her jaws to argue with them. His brown eyes were unusually hard. "Storm's one of the few dogs who kept her head cool just now. She was trying to help us—and it's obvious we needed all the help dogs could give!"

Dart, at least, looked slightly abashed, and the others fell into a surly silence, but Alpha padded to Lucky's side and solemnly watched Storm's eyes.

"All the same, Beta," she murmured. "Following Pack Law is more important than ever now. We all have to respect the hierarchy, or every dog is lost. Now is not the time for any dog to make challenges, or get ideas above her rank."

Lucky hesitated, then nodded. Storm felt her heart sink like a stone, and her tail clamped tightly between her hindlegs at the reprimand. She wanted to apologize, but no sound would come—and why, she thought with sudden anger, should she say she was sorry? The Pack had been in chaos a moment ago! She had been trying to help!

Searching the circle of dogs for a single supportive face, Storm caught Bella's eye. The look the golden-furred dog gave her was very knowing and intent, and Storm felt a small shiver in her gut. She knew exactly what Bella was telling her: *This is just the kind of thing I warned you about.*

But it was too late for Storm to argue. Without waiting for

her reply, Alpha nudged Lucky's neck, then paced forward to the center of the glade.

Into the silence, the swift-dog gave a commanding bark. "The danger has passed. It was a strange thing, seeing the loudbirds so close, but they've gone now."

"Huh." Moon gave a gruff growl. "They appeared out of nowhere, straight from the sky. That means they can do it again, at any time. How can we know the danger's truly past?"

Whisper shrank nervously closer to Storm, and Ruff and Woody exchanged glances. Beetle and Thorn stepped nearer to their mother, their expressions protective. No dog spoke.

"And if the longpaws in their bellies have loudsticks?" Moon demanded. "What would we do then? There would be no escape!"

"That's enough." Lucky bounded forward to Alpha's side, meeting Moon's angry blue eyes. "The danger *has* passed, for now at least. The best thing we can do is get back to our normal routine." He cast his gaze around them all. "*Right now.*"

Slowly, still giving themselves occasional shakes and growling softly, the dogs of the Pack began to disperse around the clearing. Rake barked to his patrol to summon them for duty. Woody nudged Sunshine to her paws, then turned to trot over to Snap, who was gathering her hunters.

"We need prey," growled Snap. "Let's get hunting. Whisper! Bella! Mickey!"

Storm stepped eagerly forward, but the hunt-dog shook her head, averting her eyes coldly. "Not you, Storm. I have enough hunters for this patrol."

Storm's tail drooped as she watched Bella, Snap and the rest of the hunters bolt away into the trees. *I was only trying to keep the Pack safe. I tried to make things better for us all.*

But in doing that, had she only made things worse for herself?

CHAPTER NINE

It had been a long day, Storm realized as she slunk through the long grass late that afternoon. She'd barely slept at all, even before that nerve-jangling encounter with the loudbirds. Her body ached with tiredness and she couldn't suppress an occasional yawn, but she was proud to be part of the special patrol Lucky had organized, and she wasn't going to let him down. After all, Bella must be tired too, she thought with a glance at Lucky's litter-sister; she'd already been out with the hunting party earlier in the day.

The meadow grass was long enough to tickle Storm's nostrils, but she wasn't worried about that. She was much more concerned with the outline ahead of her, the broken shapes of longpaw buildings that marked the edge of their deserted settlement. The very sight of the town made Storm's hackles spring erect, but she made herself pad on.

I won't let Lucky down.

"This is roughly where the loudbirds were hovering," said Lucky, raising his growl just enough for each patrol member to hear. "They did spend time over our camp, but I watched them. Mostly they seemed to be hunting for prey over the longpaw town. I think it was something particular they were hunting for—and I want to know what it was."

He's making excuses, Storm thought miserably. *He says he was watching the loudbirds while they hovered, trying to find out what they were up to. He's trying to tell us he was afraid but he didn't completely lose his senses.*

But I'm not sure I believe that. I think this time, Lucky let the Pack down.

Storm heaved a silent, unhappy sigh. Her pawsteps slowed as the patrol drew closer to the town, and around her Bella, Arrow, and Bruno walked more carefully, too. Lucky padded rapidly on, though, until Bella gave a sigh of exasperation and bounded ahead to block his way with her body.

"Beta," she growled. "Be more careful! What if there are long-paws there? The ones from the loudbirds' bellies?"

Lucky hesitated, one paw lifted. He cocked an ear at his litter-sister, and sighed. "You're right. I suppose I'm being reckless."

"And I know why." Bella gave him a sympathetic lick. "That's why we're here, isn't it?"

"What?" He looked startled.

"You feel bad because you froze when the loudbirds came. Don't look at me like that, Beta; you know it's true." She tilted her head to study his face.

Storm froze where she stood. How would Lucky react to what, in Storm's opinion, was the simple, feather-free truth? She looked from the Beta to his litter-sister and back again, licking her chops anxiously.

Bella, though, did not look the least bit wary or nervous. "Beta, you brought us out on patrol because you want to do something to make up for panicking."

Lucky's muzzle wrinkled and he averted his eyes. "I was watching the loudbirds, but I didn't want to leave Sw—Alpha."

Bella licked his ear. "That's perfectly understandable. You're going to be a Father-Dog! Of course you're going to worry about your mate and your pups. You don't have to feel bad about it."

As if embarrassed, Lucky turned toward the town again. He looked as unconvinced as Storm felt.

His main responsibility is to the Pack, and he knows it, she thought. *He's Father-Dog to all of us, in a way, just as our Alpha is our Mother-Dog. He can't think only of his mate.*

Bella was talking to her litter-brother again. "Listen, Beta, the best way to help Alpha and the pups is to do what we came here to do. Right?"

The Beta nodded, and seemed to focus properly on the task at hand. "Let's go forward carefully. Every dog on his belly. This grass is long enough to conceal us if we do it right. If there *are* any longpaws in the town, we can still avoid being spotted."

Bella obeyed immediately, followed by Storm, Arrow, and Bruno. One paw after another, they crept through the long stiff grass. It certainly did hide them, Storm thought, but it also made it hard to see. Irritated by an itch in her nose, Storm gave a muffled sneeze, then shunted another clump of grass aside with her muzzle.

There were no longpaw sounds from the town, only the tweeting of birds, the whine of wind in empty buildings, and the occasional creak and clang of loose-hanging wire. The place seemed as deserted as they'd always found it before, except . . . Storm sniffed. Through the dry bitter scent of the meadow, she could smell something else.

"Longpaws," she growled to Lucky. "Their scent is fresh. And it's pretty strong."

"Yes," he said grimly. "They've been here recently."

"I don't understand why they would come here," Bruno said, puzzled.

"I don't know, but let's get closer and find out." Lucky edged forward with caution.

Storm followed his lead, her heart crashing against her ribs. Her instincts howled at her to turn and run, but she couldn't disobey her Beta, and she didn't want to.

But she knew so little about longpaws. . . .

What happens if we meet one? she wondered. *What if it attacks? Do we attack it back?*

I'll just have to wait and take my lead from the others.

When they reached a clear track that led toward the town, all five dogs began to scent methodically at its edges, checking for longpaw traces. Still strong, realized Storm, but gradually fading. The longpaws might have been here recently, but it seemed they'd left.

Storm paused, pawing at a deep, dark groove of mud in the grass. "What's this? It doesn't look like a mark of the Big Growl."

Bella trotted back to her. "No, that's not damage from the Growl. Ah. Look, there are two ruts. A loudcage has been here."

"One with very large paws," added Bruno, tilting his head to examine the deeply scored marks. The raw earth looked damp, and there were strange patterns etched into it.

Lucky and Arrow had joined them now, too, sniffing at the

scars. "Yes," said Lucky, "and these marks are fresh, too. A huge loudcage cut across the grass quite recently."

"But why?" murmured Arrow.

Good question! Storm looked expectantly at Lucky—didn't he always know how the longpaws' strange minds worked?—but he only shook his head in perplexity. Storm felt a tremor of unease. If Lucky couldn't explain this, what dog could?

Staying closer together, the dogs crept into the town with trepidation, bristling at every strange scent. As they rounded a sharp corner onto a stretch of hardstone path, Lucky took a breath.

"More loudcages," he murmured, "but they're not moving."

"They're asleep," said Bruno, staring at the massive shapes of the slumbering monsters. "Let's move very quietly."

Storm found it hard to breathe as she stepped trembling between the first two giant creatures. Each had a single huge fang, poised in the air as if ready to bite down; she was glad that the monsters were sleeping. But they had already done their damage. There were deep, ragged wounds in the hardstone, and the walls of some of the longpaw houses had been torn into careful piles of rubble. *That's not the work of the Big Growl*, thought Storm with a shiver. *The loudcages ripped down those longpaw homes, and they dug those great gashes in the hardstone, too.* The wounds looked so deep, Storm knew the Earth-Dog must be hurting.

What were these longpaws up to?

As the dogs came to a halt between the dozing loudcages, Lucky pricked his ears, scanning the road ahead of them. "I'm not sure we should go much farther."

Arrow's fur rippled visibly with a tremor of anxiety. "These loudcages might be guarding something, but I don't want to be here when they wake up," he muttered.

"And there are others, farther on," said Bruno. "They look almost as big."

Storm couldn't express her own opinion; her throat was tight with fear, but she knew she'd rather saunter into a giantfur's den than walk between more of these gigantic loudcages.

Bella narrowed her eyes, thoughtful. "If any longpaws jumped out and surprised us, escape would be difficult in this place. We could be hemmed in among the loudcages."

"True," agreed Lucky. "We'll go back to the camp and report to Alpha. I think we've seen enough."

A wave of relief made Storm dizzy, and she spun on her haunches to begin the retreat, but Bruno's desolate voice stopped her in her tracks.

"Are we going to have to move on again?" he whined.

Turning back, Storm saw that his head was drooping with unhappiness.

"It took us so long to find our camp," the big dog went on, glancing longingly in the direction of their forest. "It's our territory!" He licked his chops, and an element of resentful loathing crept into his voice. "We fought off *Fierce Dogs* to claim it."

Storm bristled at the tone of his growl, and she saw Arrow's hackles spring up too. She caught her fellow Fierce Dog's narrowed eyes, and knew he was thinking what she was thinking.

Does Bruno despise us, then?

Lucky had hunched his golden shoulders. "I understand, Bruno. Nobody wants to move on again. But longpaws and giant loudcages—and loudbirds? Seems to me they're an even tougher enemy than Blade's Pack. We may not have a choice."

Storm felt misery rise in her throat, and her ears and tail drooped. "We came so far to get here, Beta."

"Yes, Storm, but—"

An abrupt whine interrupted them, and Storm turned with surprise to look at Arrow. He had stiffened, and he took a backward step, his sharp nostrils flaring. Then he paced forward, his

SURVIVORS: THE GATHERING DARKNESS

pointed ears pricked as high as they could go.

"Arrow!" Lucky was startled. "What's wrong?"

There was a low, agonized growl in Arrow's throat. In a choked voice he said, "It's Ripper."

Storm jerked back in surprise. *Ripper was one of Blade's dogs!*

Surely Ripper had fled with the rest of Blade's Pack after the battle? But Arrow must know her scent, and if she really was here, then there could be big trouble.

Blade's Pack wanted to kill me. And if any of them survived, they might still be clinging to her wish. . . .

With a suddenness that took them all by surprise, Arrow sprang forward and bolted between the sleeping loudcages.

"Arrow, come back!" barked Lucky.

He might as well have been calling to the Wind-Dogs. Arrow streaked around a corner and vanished into the town's deserted streets. Bella made to bound after him, but Lucky nipped her haunches to stop her. She turned, annoyed.

"That's not a good idea, Bella," growled Lucky.

Bella's muzzle curled. "We can't let him go alone! What if he runs into one of Blade's dogs? What if it's a trap?"

Lucky hesitated, uncertain, and Bella took her chance to shove her snout close to his.

"Arrow's one of us now," she barked. "We need to back him up!"

Lucky closed his eyes briefly and sighed. "All right."

"Not me," yelped Bruno angrily. "If that creature wants to go dashing off in search of his Fierce Dog friends, let him deal with the consequences!"

Storm gaped at him, hurt, but Bella didn't even pause to argue. "Fine," she snapped, and bounded off in the direction Arrow had taken. Without hesitation, Lucky and Storm followed at her haunches.

As they darted nervously between the loudcages, Storm felt her heart grow heavy as a stone. Arrow's scent was easy to follow, but finding him in this web of streets would be a dangerous job. What if he *had* run straight into enemy dogs—or even longpaws?

As they raced around the corner after him, though, she realized her worry had been unfounded. Arrow stood right there, stock-still beside a thin stream of dirty water that ran along the edge of the hardstone path. His head was bowed, and Storm saw what lay beneath him.

The corpse of a dog.

For a wild moment Storm wondered if Arrow had killed some enemy in a swift, sudden battle. But, she realized as the three of them slowed to approach Arrow, the body was not fresh.

A black-and-tan Fierce Dog lay sprawled in the gutter, her once-glossy coat now dull and lifeless, her ribs and hip-bones jutting beneath it. Pale worms crawled at her empty eyes, and squirmed on her lolling, swollen tongue; they had been feeding on her for some time. The smell of death was overpowering, and Storm couldn't repress a huge shudder.

"Ripper," said Arrow softly.

A creeping horror turned Storm's blood cold, but it was mingled with guilty relief. If Ripper *had* still nursed Blade's mad ambition to kill Storm, there was nothing she could ever do about it now. Stepping across the dirty runnel of water to stand next to Arrow, Storm glanced into his eyes.

The terrible sadness in them was unsettling. Arrow gave her a brief, sidelong look, then said softly, "Not every dog in Blade's Pack was evil."

The tremor of guilt shuddered through Storm again. *Did he know what I was thinking?* But before she could open her jaws to console the other Fierce Dog, she heard a gruff, hard-edged voice behind them.

"You could have fooled me."

Bruno stood behind them. The burly dog had followed after

all, and his eyes were cold as he glared at Arrow and the dead Ripper. Then he slanted them at Storm.

Storm stiffened. A growl rose in her throat, but she swallowed it. *Bruno's not talking about me. He can't be! I was never part of Blade's Pack.*

Although, she realized with a jolt, Bruno had never really liked her. . . .

Bruno had always judged her first and foremost as a Fierce Dog. He might tolerate her, but she had always had to prove herself and her goodwill, every pawstep of the way. Shivering with resentment, Storm took a sidelong step closer to Arrow.

But Arrow didn't rise to Bruno's taunt, either. Calmly he gazed into the burly dog's hostile eyes. "We're not like Wild Dogs," he said. "We're not even like you Leashed Dogs. You're born with your nature, or you grow into it. You *decide* what you are." He paused to glance down at Ripper. "Not us Fierce Dogs. Our nature is made for us, by the longpaw Masters."

"That can't be true," began Bella.

"I didn't see much of it," Arrow admitted with a sigh. "I was born not long before the Big Growl, when the Masters fled and left us. But I do have some memories. I saw Fierce Dogs being marched around the Dog-Garden, over and over again, drilled to be obedient. I didn't understand what the Masters were saying to them, of course, but they were always angry. They never spoke except in an angry bark. They'd strike any dog, too, if they put a paw wrong—even pups."

Storm tilted her head, filled with sympathy. It surprised her that there wasn't a trace of anger in Arrow's soft voice. His puphood sounded awful, yet the way Arrow talked, it sounded as if he *missed* it.

Would I have been as vicious as the other Fierce Dogs, wondered Storm, *if I'd been raised in the Dog-Garden by the Masters? Would they have given me the nature they wanted me to have?*

She couldn't imagine what it had been like to be raised and drilled by the Masters, and she didn't want to. Blade had been as cruel and stern as any longpaw could ever be; had they made her that way, turned her into a dog version of themselves?

Thank the Spirit Dogs I was raised by Lucky and Martha. She shivered. *Even if some of the Pack Dogs don't trust me, at least I had a choice. At least I was free to become my own dog.*

But Arrow had been brought up in the Dog-Garden. Arrow *had* known the Masters, even if it had only been for a short time, and his nature had been shaped by them. He was a true Fierce Dog. . . .

Unease fluttered in Storm's gut. In the silence, she heard

Bruno's low sullen growl. "We can't trust a Fierce Dog."

No other dog had heard that, she realized, and she wasn't about to cause a fight by challenging Bruno—not right here and now.

But was the burly Fight Dog right, anyway?

Could the Pack really, truly trust Arrow?

CHAPTER TEN

Storm hadn't felt so contentedly drowsy in a long time. For once, she thought, she might get a good night's rest; her belly felt full and her head heavy with sleep. All around the camp, dogs chatted quietly or half dozed in the evening light.

Just as Storm was about to nestle into her warm, leafy sleeping quarters, Sunshine spoke, her fluffy white tail waving. "Tell us another story about the Wind-Dogs, Alpha? I haven't been able to stop thinking about them."

Bella gave a short amused bark: "Do you still need a pup-tale to go to sleep, Omega? Don't be silly."

A few other dogs scoffed as well, their jaws gaping into lazy grins. Lucky raised his head, but before he could speak, Alpha got to her feet and walked slowly and deliberately to the center of the clearing. Her bark of summons rang through the clear evening air, making Storm raise her head and prick an ear.

"My Pack! Gather around. I have something important to say about the Spirit Dogs who guide us."

Storm padded into the center of the clearing with the rest of the Pack as they formed their circle. Every dog but the small regular evening patrol was present, and it struck Storm how large their Pack was growing. The dogs pressed flank to flank, alert for their Alpha to begin speaking. Lucky stood at his mate's side, gazing at her supportively, his expression a mixture of respect and adoration.

Alpha turned her slim head to meet the eyes of each dog, then nodded with satisfaction.

"I know there are dogs in this Pack who don't believe in the Wind-Dogs," she declared, "and I respect that. It's not easy to accept new Spirit Dogs when you have never heard their tales before. Accepting their influence is even harder." She looked kindly on the Pack. "But I have this to say: I want you all to respect my beliefs in turn. The Wind-Dogs are real to me, and they are important in my life. They are as real to me"—she glanced lovingly at her Beta—"as Beta's Forest-Dog is to him. I won't force you to believe in them, or try to prove to you that the Wind-Dogs are real. All that matters is that I believe, and I know they are with me."

Storm heard low murmurs of approval go through at least some of the Pack, and Daisy bounced onto her four paws. "I hope they are real!" she exclaimed, her tail wagging hard. "We could use more Spirit Dogs on our side. We have lots of mouths to feed, don't we? The more Spirit Dogs there are to help us, the better!"

Woody gave a shake of his head at that, frowning slightly. "Too many mouths? I hope that's not a dig at us." He nodded at Twitch and the other former members of his Pack. "You dogs of the old Pack can't go on blaming everything on us. After all, we *chose* to fight with you against the Fierce Dogs. And we *chose* to accept your invitation to stay."

Alpha stood up to give a commanding bark, and scraped the earth with a paw. "No more quarreling!"

Woody fell silent, and so did the other muttering dogs. Daisy, though, grumbled under her breath.

"I wasn't pointing paws at *any* dog. Just stating a fact." Sulkily she flopped onto her belly.

Alpha eased herself carefully onto her side, making room for her plump stomach. "I mean what I say. I won't force stories of the Wind-Dogs on you. But I want to know that the Pack respects my beliefs."

Again the ripple of agreement went through the Pack. Storm

pricked her ears and watched her Packmates in wonder. *Life's so different with Sweet as Alpha.* Under their previous Alpha, the savage half wolf, the dogs would have been made to believe. Or at least, they'd have been barked at until they *said* they believed. And if they hadn't, they'd have found themselves without a share of the prey pile until they changed their minds.

That's not how Sweet does things, thought Storm happily. *I like the change.*

A small, white fluffy shape got to her paws at the edge of the circle. Sunshine wagged her dirty plume of a tail, and cleared her throat shyly.

"I'd still like to hear a story of the Wind-Dogs right now," she told the circle in a small, respectful voice. "I'm really interested! Could you tell us one, Alpha?"

For long moments the Pack was silent, surprised, but then the yips of agreement began to rise.

"A story would be fun!" barked Daisy.

Woody nodded his matted brown-and-cream head. "I don't mind hearing a story. I can make my own mind up as to whether I believe it."

"Yes, I think we'd all like to hear," agreed Mickey.

"Go ahead, Alpha!" growled Dart.

But Woody, Storm noticed, was the only member of Twitch's Pack to speak up. The rest of them kept a firm, though respectful, silence, as the former Leashed Dogs and Sweet's old Pack whined their enthusiasm. Bella, too, did not speak.

Daisy was still bouncing with excitement. "What if a Wind-Dog stumbles, Alpha? That's what I want to know. They run so fast after the Golden Deer, surely they must slip and fall sometimes!" Her eyes were full of bright curiosity.

Alpha gave a contented, gruff laugh. "It's certainly happened, Daisy. Sometimes a Wind-Dog does miss her pawsteps. When that happens, and she stumbles, the gust of her fall is powerful enough to knock dogs to the ground. You can hear her yelp and whine, angry at herself. Or you might hear her howl to her Pack-mates, telling them she'll catch up with them soon."

Rake gave a skeptical yip, curling his scarred muzzle. "So why does the wind grow more fierce *after* Long Light, when the Wind-Dogs have already caught the Golden Deer? Hm?"

Storm glanced nervously at their Alpha, wondering how she'd react to the mockery in Rake's voice. But she looked unperturbed, and her calm expression didn't change.

"Oh, the Wind-Dogs take the capture of the Golden Deer very seriously. When they're not hunting it, they are racing one another in preparation. They need to practice until they are faster than she is. And so the winds blow even fiercer when Long Light is over."

Mickey nodded. "That makes sense to me."

"Not to me," grumbled Rake, but very quietly.

"Imagine if we could catch a Golden Deer on the ground," whined Daisy dreamily.

"Well," laughed Snap, "that would certainly make the Wind-Dogs pleased with us."

"It could bring us great good fortune," agreed Bruno thoughtfully.

Sunshine was whirling in a circle, bumping into other dogs in her excitement. Mickey dodged back as her fluffy tail whipped across his muzzle. "I *can't* imagine it, Daisy! That's what makes it so exciting! Oh, let's catch a Golden Deer!"

Rake's irritated bark cut through the excited yelps. "What's wrong with all of you? You're so keen to believe in these Wind-Dogs, but not one of you takes the Fear-Dog seriously. And you should! He's the one who rules the Sky-Dogs, after all. Terror told us so!"

One or two dogs opened their jaws angrily to argue, but it was Arrow who stepped into the center of the group. Storm was struck again by his calm, diffident demeanor.

"Maybe the Spirit Dogs aren't separate beings at all," he suggested. "Have you thought of that? It could be that different Packs come up with different names for the same Spirit Dogs. When I lived in the Dog-Garden under the Masters, the older members of my pack spoke of a Watch-Dog. He sounds a bit like your Fear-Dog, Rake. I was told then that all the Sky-Dogs respect and serve the Watch-Dog."

Arrow tilted his head at the Pack, but his words were met with silence. Some dogs gaped at him, some exchanged skeptical looks, but none spoke. After a moment his ears drooped, and he licked his jaws sheepishly and shifted from side to side.

"Sorry," he muttered as he shuffled backward into the circle of dogs. "It was just an idea. You know. That maybe we all believe in the same dogs."

Storm felt her heart turn over for Arrow. What had taken the other dogs aback—his theory of the Spirit Dogs, or the fact he'd had the nerve to speak at all? Certainly Breeze was letting out a low growl as she glared at him.

Twitch coughed a bark. "Why all this talk of invisible dogs? Maybe we should forget about them for a while. Concentrate on important things, like *hunting*."

Snap looked at him in astonishment. "But Twitch, we have to respect the Spirit Dogs!"

"Why?" He hunched his shoulders. "What have the Spirit Dogs ever done for us? They never actually show up in a crisis, do they?"

Around him there were whines of horrified protest.

"The Forest-Dog brings us prey!" exclaimed Mickey, with a respectful glance at Lucky.

"And Martha had a very special relationship with the River-Dog," put in Storm, with a pang of memory.

"The Sun-Dog warms our days," said Moon firmly, "and the Moon-Dog gives us light in the darkness."

"And we can *see* the Sky-Dogs when they battle!" yelped Daisy, as if that settled the matter. "We can see Lightning himself as he jumps to Earth!"

The moment of unity warmed Storm's heart; it was good to see the Pack put aside petty differences to agree on the benevolence of the Spirit Dogs.

"Of course the Spirit Dogs are real." Lucky spoke up with firmness. "How else do you explain my dreams about the Storm of Dogs? They came true."

"Don't forget that the Earth-Dog takes all dogs when they

die," added Chase, with a severe look at his former leader.

"Wait a moment." The voice was Bella's, and she took a pace forward into the circle. "Why are we so keen to believe those are Spirits? Maybe Twitch is right. There's a Sun all right, and a Moon, and the Earth, and the Forest. We can't deny that, but perhaps they don't *help* dogs at all. Maybe they're just *there*. And maybe they don't think or have feelings at all!"

"Well, wait a moment," blurted Twitch, looking unsettled as he scratched awkwardly at his ear. "I didn't go quite that far. . . ."

The barks and calls and yelps faded to silence as the Pack fidgeted, some of them a little shamefaced. A dog's claws scratched against pebbles. There was the sound of another shaking his shaggy coat. Otherwise, there was only the sigh of wind in the branches above them.

Who won that argument? thought Storm uneasily, and she swallowed hard.

I'm not sure any dog did.

It was rather reassuring to be in the woods they'd once called Twitch's Forest when she was actually *supposed* to be there, Storm thought wryly. For once she hadn't woken up here, disoriented by darkness and bad dreams, but had come as one of a loose hunting group, all hunting separately at the moment. This time she was wide awake and filled with energy, all her senses alert for prey as she bounded through the undergrowth.

And also, if she was honest, keeping half an eye open for a Golden Deer...

She couldn't explain it even to herself, but she was desperately eager to see the magical creature for herself. Perhaps it was just that she wanted living proof of the Spirit Dogs, before her eyes, so maybe if she wished hard enough, the Spirit Dogs themselves would reveal the Golden Deer to her? She breathed a silent plea to the invisible Spirits as she ran.

Please, Sky-Dogs, I just want to know...

Something gold flickered at the corner of her eye, and Storm gasped, nearly tripping over her own paws. Standing still, her neck fur rising, she stared at the spot.

It could have been a claw of sunlight hitting a wet leaf. But what if it wasn't?

If there was a chance it could have been the Deer, she had to make sure. She couldn't reject the Spirit Dogs, not when they might have answered her so swiftly.

Stealthily, placing her paws with care, Storm crept through the sun-dappled forest. She could be an impatient hunter, she knew, but not this time; she followed her senses with all the delicacy she could manage, as if she was tracking the quickest and most jittery of prey.

Pressing her flank against a rough tree trunk, she held still and listened hard. Her nostrils flared, searching the still air, but then she realized: *I don't even know what the Golden Deer smells like. No dog does.*

Except for the Wind-Dogs . . .

The Golden Deer could be close, just a rabbit-chase away, and she wouldn't know it. Would a live Golden Deer, a shadow of the prey the Wind Dogs chased, smell like a real deer? Her ears drooped. Surely the Wind-Dogs would not mask the Deer's scent? Or were they too jealous of their prey to let an earthbound dog catch even an earthly shadow of it? Maybe Sweet was wrong, and an ordinary dog catching a Golden Deer wouldn't please the Wind-Dogs one bit.

Or maybe Rake's right. Maybe there are no Wind-Dogs.

Easing her body away from the tree, Storm shook herself. She wouldn't dwell on Rake's wild claims; after all, he was a dog who believed in the Fear-Dog! Sweet was her Alpha, and if Sweet believed in the Wind-Dogs, then Storm would too.

But why can't I feel so much as a breeze right now?

Her gut turned over as she realized: *Maybe it's because I'm here. The Wind-Dogs want nothing to do with me. Is that it?*

She hoped not. Swallowing, she turned and began to pick her way through the scrubby grass, back toward the camp. Perhaps if she hunted somewhere else she'd have better luck; and maybe she'd forget her wild hopes of seeing the elusive Golden Deer in favor of some living, breathing rabbits.

She took a leap over a tussock of grass, only to career into a smaller dog coming the other way, and knock him flying. "Whisper!"

The little dog scrambled to his paws and shook himself, looking embarrassed. "Don't worry, Storm."

"I'm sorry." She stood still, mortified by her clumsiness. "I was a bit distracted—I didn't pick up your scent."

"Honestly, it's fine." Whisper raised a hindpaw to scratch a twig out of his ear fur. "I know you didn't mean it."

Storm's skin tingled with irritation. Did Whisper really have to be so nice all the time? "Well, I was clumsy and I'm sorry."

"All right, Storm," he said cheerfully. "Are you going back to camp?"

"Ye . . . es . . . I thought I might hunt on the way, but—"

"I'll come with you." He turned and trotted at her flank. "What did you think of all that talk last night? It was odd, I thought. I've never heard dogs argue about whether the Spirit Dogs exist."

"Things change. Dogs get new ideas," she told him a little grumpily. Then she sighed and snapped idly at a branch. "But I think maybe they just needed something to argue about."

"Oh, do you really think so? I hope the Pack doesn't fall apart," he said. "It's not good to squabble for the sake of it, is it?" He didn't give her time to answer, she noticed with exasperation. "I mean, Wind-Dogs, Fear-Dogs . . . who cares which ones are real? We should just believe in the Spirits we want to believe in, like Alpha said. Except the Fear-Dog can't be very powerful, can he? Even if he *is* real."

"Well, you never know," began Storm nervously. They were at the edge of the camp by now—she'd been jogging fast to make the one-sided conversation with Whisper as short as possible—and she didn't want to set off another argument among the Pack.

"But we do know!" yelped Whisper, bounding over a mossy rock and into the glade. "The Fear-Dog probably isn't real, and if he is, he can't do much. He's feeble, if you ask me!"

"I wish you'd keep your voice down." Storm glanced at the group of dogs who were watching them with their ears pinned back. Woody had his head cocked, Snap was eyeing Whisper with slight contempt, and Breeze, Rake, and Ruff were staring with their muzzles curled. Even Sunshine, trotting out of Alpha's den with old bedding in her mouth, looked a little surprised to hear Whisper barking so loudly.

Whisper didn't seem to notice or care. "I mean, look at the way you got rid of Terror! If the Fear-Dog was meant to be looking after him, he didn't do a very good job, did he? So much for the all-powerful Fear-Dog!" Whisper's tongue was lolling, his eyes shining as he gazed at Storm. "I'm glad you beat Terror. You're stronger than his horrible Fear-Dog!"

Storm could not cross the glade fast enough, and when she fell in with another group of hunters, Whisper was finally forced to drop away. He gave her a last cheerful yelp of farewell, and padded off toward his own den.

Storm's skin felt hot with embarrassment beneath her fur. *I don't miss Terror*, she thought, *and I'm glad he's dead. But I hate remembering what I did.*

What I had *to do.*

She knew one thing for sure: The way Whisper went on about it, eyes shining whenever he mentioned Storm's heroic act of glorious warfare, was not helping her reputation with the Pack. . . .

CHAPTER ELEVEN

Storm yawned, blinking at the Sun-Dog. He had padded close to the horizon and now he was curling up in his end-of-day red-and-golden glow. Why, she wondered, did the Sun-Dog wait until he was almost asleep before he stretched out and showed his most beautiful colors? The ways of the Spirit Dogs were very mysterious.

She laid her head on her paws and watched as the rest of the Pack gathered around the prey pile. Lucky seemed anxious tonight, pacing back and forth and fussing around Alpha as she plodded heavily from their den to the center of the glade.

"You must be tired, Alpha. Stay in our den. Let me bring you your prey-share there. . . ."

"Certainly not," barked Alpha irritably. "I'm carrying pups, not the weight of the Earth-Dog. And I'm not on my way to join her, either. I'm perfectly all right, Beta, and I'm not helpless."

"Of course not, Alpha." Lucky wagged his tail fondly. "Sorry I—"

He didn't manage to finish his apology. A wild barking and snarling erupted from the far side of the clearing. *Right by Moon's den!* realized Storm with a bolt of dread.

"What's going on?" snapped Alpha. "What's this noise about?"

Storm jumped to her paws, her tail stiff and her hackles bristling. A crowd of dogs had gathered at the entrance to Moon's den, and as Lucky trotted rapidly toward the commotion, Storm fell in at his flank. She stayed close to him as he nosed and shouldered his way through the throng of dogs. Pushing Chase aside, shoving past Dart, he finally broke out to the clear semicircle in front of the den entrance. Storm squeezed through behind him.

Breeze stood there, her head low, shoulders hunched, snarling at Moon. Between them, stuffed beneath a pile of dry leaves and twigs, lay scraps of food: a rabbit's haunch, two dead voles, a headless squirrel.

Lucky stared at Breeze, then at Moon. "What's going on?" he barked.

Breeze tipped back her head as if she could no longer contain her howl of fury. "Moon has been stealing prey! Hoarding it!"

Moon? Steal food? "I don't believe it," blurted Storm. She felt

Lucky nip her shoulder, and she took a quick step away from him, shocked.

"What kind of a Pack dog is she?" yelped Breeze angrily.

Moon bounded a pace closer to Lucky. "I didn't do this, Beta! You can't believe I would, surely? I have no idea how that prey got there!"

Her protest was howled down by a volley of barks and snarls from the watching dogs.

"Typical!" barked Woody. "It's Alpha's Pack again, thinking the rules don't apply to them."

Chase growled. "Where's the honor in hoarding prey?"

"Letting the rest of the Pack go hungry!" added Ruff in a high howl.

Storm's gut churned in anger at the unfairness of it. "No!" she barked, unable to contain herself. "You can't say that about Alpha's Pack! We are honorable dogs and we would never do such a thing. And that includes Moon!"

"Every dog calm down," growled Lucky, with a particularly sharp look at Storm.

"What is going on?" The press of dogs gave way as Alpha stalked through them, her ears pricked.

"Don't worry, Alpha." Lucky nuzzled the swift-dog's shoulder.

"I'll handle this. I don't want you being put under any stress."

Alpha, Storm was sure, rolled her eyes. Ignoring Lucky, she glared at Moon. "Explain yourself," she growled.

Moon swallowed, then clenched her jaws determinedly and shot angry glances around Twitch's former Packmates. "Alpha, I promise you. I have *no idea* how this food came to be here. Why would I do something so stupid, never mind shameful?"

"I'm certainly willing to give you the benefit of the doubt, Moon." Alpha's eyes were hard. "So tell me: Who did it? Can you point a paw at the culprit?"

Storm pricked her ears forward, eagerly waiting for Moon's response.

Moon licked her jaws, then opened them to speak. She shut them again with a snap. At last she averted her angry eyes from Alpha's.

"No, Alpha. I have no idea who could have done this: just that it wasn't me."

"Did you see anything suspicious? Any dog behaving oddly around your den?"

Moon shook her head. "I saw nothing," she growled. "Whoever it was, they were too clever for me." She glared at Ruff's smug face, then at Rake.

Storm's gut clenched. *The way she's looking at them . . . does Moon suspect they're responsible?* Storm glanced in horror at Ruff and Rake. *Surely they would never do such a thing . . . and yet some dog did. . . .*

"So you can't accuse any other dog, Moon?" Alpha lowered her head to stare keenly at the proud white-and-black dog.

"I can't accuse any dog, no," snarled Moon. "Because I don't know who it was, and *I* don't want to fling false accusations. That would only make more trouble." She stiffened her shoulders, and drew herself up to sweep her gaze around at all the watching dogs—but most of all, Twitch's former Pack. "But I vow to the Spirit Dogs, Alpha, that I *will* find out. And that dog will know my vengeance, and—"

"Be quiet." Alpha's voice was low and silky, and it silenced Moon immediately. "If you can't explain how the prey came to be here, then you must take responsibility. You know what that means, Moon. You leave me no choice."

Moon's angry defiance had melted into misery as her Alpha spoke. Her head drooped, and her tail clung to her haunches. "Yes, Alpha," she growled. "I must be punished for something I *did not do.*"

Storm's jaw felt slack. Staring at Alpha and Moon in disbelief, she thought: *This can't be happening. Moon's innocent, but she's going to accept the punishment anyway!*

If such an injustice was inflicted on her, Storm knew, she'd never cower to the ground and take it. She'd show her fury with teeth and claws, and every dog would know never to dare do such a thing again. *Yet Moon is ducking her tail to this.*

With a stirring of faint hope, she glanced toward Alpha. *She won't punish Moon—she can't!*

Alpha shook her head slowly. Her slim face was impassive, Storm realized, aghast. *I don't know if Sweet believes any of this or not, but if Moon can't prove her innocence . . .*

With Alpha's next calm words, Storm's fears were realized. "For this crime you'll eat last today, Moon. Even Omega will fill her belly before you do. And you will continue to eat last until I tell you to reclaim your place."

"She shouldn't eat at all," said Breeze in a low, resentful snarl.

"That's enough," snapped Alpha. "She will eat last of all the Pack, and, starting tomorrow, Moon, you will take High Watch. I expect to see you on the cliffs before Sun-Dog rises, and you will watch through the day and night for longpaws and for loudbirds, especially any that come from the direction of the Endless Lake. You will remain there until I am sure you have learned to respect Pack Law. Make sure you are vigilant, and you will repay the Pack the debt of honor you owe us."

Shocked speechless, Storm turned to Lucky, but he shifted his gaze to the ground. *Avoid my eyes if you like, Beta*, she thought grimly, *but I know you're as unhappy about this as I am!* High Watch would be terrible for Moon; the cliffs were swept by constant fierce winds, and if it rained, she'd be battered and soaked.

Storm wanted to bark her outrage and disbelief, but Alpha was already turning away to stalk back to her den. The mob of dogs parted before her, quieted by her silent fury, and Lucky padded after her.

Try as she might, Storm could not shake her anger at the injustice of Moon's punishment, and when the Pack gathered to share their prey, it only stoked her feelings. The other dogs were calm at last, almost nonchalant—presumably, she thought sourly, because they felt Alpha had properly dealt with Moon and the stolen food. Storm, though, could barely eat; her appetite was crushed, her mouth felt dry, and the prey tasted bitter. She'd rather have given her whole portion to Moon—yet she was almost as furious with Moon as she was with Alpha and the rest of the Pack. *How can she take this so passively?*

Surreptitiously, Storm eyed the rest of the Pack. Who could possibly have stolen food and framed Moon for it? Which dog would *want* to? She searched their faces desperately for any sign of guilt or remorse, yet all she could see was a Pack riven by confusion and distrust. Some of Twitch's old Pack glared at Moon with distaste; some even shook their heads in disgust. The old members of Sweet's Pack looked more distressed than angry, as if they were actually entertaining the idea that their old friend might be guilty. Storm's hackles shivered.

The trouble, she realized dismally, was that she had no idea who might have framed Moon—because there were too many candidates. Small rivalries, niggling enmities, and discontentment had been brewing since the Packs united, and though it might all have been sternly repressed by Alpha and Lucky, it had had the chance to grow unseen. Beneath the surface of their daily lives the problems had grown like tiny shoots into thick, twisted roots, and now they threatened to undermine the life of the whole Pack.

Was there a dog who was intentionally feeding all this anger? Some dog must have meant to stir up more distrust by hiding the prey in Moon's den.

That has to be what it is, Storm thought with a sickening bolt of realization. *There's a schemer in the camp—some dog happy to create conflict, to get other dogs into trouble. How can we ever thrive and be happy with a traitor among us?*

The small squirrel she had eaten felt like a lump of stone in her stomach. With her head on her paws, she lay watching her Packmates as they took their turns choosing prey from the pile. The heap was diminishing steadily, and Storm feared there would be almost nothing left by the time Moon's turn came around. Twitch's former comrades, in particular, seemed to take pleasure tonight in gulping down large portions. Still, there was a rabbit haunch left when they'd finished, and a small mouse. Perhaps Moon's portion wouldn't be so small after all.

"Omega." Alpha's tail thumped on the ground as her gaze fell on the little white dog. "You may eat."

Sunshine's round black eyes widened as she licked her lips and padded nervously forward. *She can't have had the chance to eat this much since she was with her longpaws,* thought Storm, with a pang of pity for the little Omega. *She at least deserves to eat well tonight. That's one good thing in all of this.*

Sunshine, though, seemed nervous and hesitant. She pawed the mouse, and tore a small bite from it. Gulping it down, she took one more mouthful, then stepped back, her tail wagging slowly.

"That was good," she whined. "I'm full now, Alpha. Thank you."

Alpha stiffened slightly, raising herself up on her forepaws. "Omega!"

"Really, I'm—"

"Do not lie to me, Omega. I am your Alpha." There was a severe glint in the swift-dog's eyes. "Pack rules are Pack rules, and Moon has broken them. Do not do the same yourself. You *will* eat your fill, Omega, or you will be punished too."

Sunshine shifted from one paw to the other, whimpering sadly under her breath, but no dog spoke up to defend her. At last she whined softly, "But Alpha, I'm only a little dog. So I only need a little food. And I'm used to not eating much. Moon shouldn't be weak, for the Pack's sake, so letting her go hungry doesn't make sense, and—"

"That is *enough*," barked Alpha, lifting her slender head to glare at Sunshine. The little dog cowered, shivering. "Bad dogs must be punished; Alphas are to be obeyed. That is *Pack Law!* Unless you want to go without food altogether, Omega, you *will* stop arguing with me, and you *will* eat your fill!"

For a long, horrible heartbeat, there was silence in the glade. Then, still quivering, Sunshine crept forward to the prey pile again. She took the last rabbit-haunch in her jaws and began to chew and gulp.

To Storm, it was clear poor Sunshine was having to force the meat down, and her gut twisted with pity. There was no doubt

Sunshine was hungry, and this would be the first time in many journeys of the Moon-Dog that the little Omega had had a full belly. But she wasn't able to enjoy it. Eating the food that should have been Moon's looked like it was only making her utterly miserable.

When Sunshine had finally choked down the last possible mouthful, all that was left for Moon was a little more than half a mouse. The spark of annoyance in Storm's belly was warming into pure rage. When every dog had stretched, yawned and padded off to his den, she continued to lie on the edge of the clearing, seething.

This is hopeless! She scraped impatiently at the ground with her foreclaws. *I can't just sulk here all night, but I won't sleep till I've confronted them.*

Hauling herself onto her paws, she paced determinedly over the damp grass toward Lucky and Alpha's den. But before she reached the overhanging branches that sheltered the entrance, she saw Lucky's shape emerge from the shadows, starlight gleaming on his golden fur. Storm halted, and waited for him, her ears laid flat against her skull.

"What is it, Storm?" he sighed as he padded up to face her. "I could smell how upset you are from all the way across the clearing, but Alpha needs her rest. Can we talk privately?"

Storm took a breath, then grunted in agreement. "All right, Beta."

"Good. Follow me." Lucky turned and slunk between the trees, his tail low.

Storm followed as he led her to a small rocky dip between two clusters of pines by the freshwater pond. Lucky turned to her and sat on his haunches, still and grave, and waited.

"Lucky," Storm said at last, glaring at the pines behind him, "I'm sorry, I really am. I don't want to cause trouble, and I don't want to disturb Alpha just now, but—I can't help it. This whole business is unfair, and it's not right. Moon's innocent! Why can't you and Alpha see that?"

Lucky watched her for a long moment. He tilted his head thoughtfully, and his tail tapped the ground. Finally he gave a heavy sigh.

"Storm, I know she's innocent."

She couldn't help gasping, and her eyes widened. "You *know?*"

"Of course I do," he told her irritably, "and so does Alpha. At least, we're as sure as we can be without any evidence. Moon's better than that."

Storm felt as if he'd butted her hard in the belly. "So, why did you—"

The sound in Lucky's throat was half whine, half growl, and all frustration. "Because rules are rules, Storm, and Pack Law is Pack Law! Surely you can see that? The food was by her den, and where's the evidence against any other dog?"

"But . . ." Storm licked her chops nervously. "But you *know* some dog put it there, just to get her into trouble."

"*Which* dog, Storm? Moon was the only dog implicated." He gave a sigh of impatience. "If Sweet—if *Alpha* overlooked this, if she went easy on Moon because she *knows* her better, how would that look to the others? It would just prove those dogs right who say that she favors her original Pack. The dogs of Twitch's Pack would be furious, and how would that benefit Pack unity? Things would be even worse than they are now." Dryly he added, "And that's bad enough."

Storm whined softly. "It just doesn't seem fair, Lucky. To punish a dog you know has done nothing."

"We don't have a choice, Storm. You know that, if you'd cool your hot head and think about it. As a matter of fact, Alpha and I were talking about this just before you tried to barge in." He gave her a rueful tilt of his head. "She hates doing this to Moon as much as I do. As much as *you* hate it. But she has to be a fair and consistent Alpha—and more than that, she has to *prove* that she is.

What happens tomorrow, if one of Twitch's Pack does something bad and earns a punishment? Will they think that should be overlooked too? Or if Alpha does punish that dog anyway, will they think she's only doing it because he's one of Twitch's dogs? We can't start making distinctions between the Packs, Storm. That would end in disaster. And haven't we all seen more than enough disaster?"

Storm met Lucky's eyes. They were gazing directly into hers now, brown and clear, but as she tilted her head and looked closer, she knew he wasn't telling her the truth. Not the whole truth, anyway.

She licked her jaws. "All of that is words, Lucky. Just words. You're quoting Pack Law at me, but you don't really believe it. There's something else on your mind." She focused hard on his open, honest-seeming eyes, and Lucky took a breath and looked away.

"All right," he grunted. "There is something else. I'll tell you, Storm, but it goes no further."

"Of course." She barked out the words, annoyed that he felt he had to say that. "What is it, Lucky?"

"This whole thing . . . Moon being framed for something she didn't do. It bothers me even more than it bothers you, and do you know why?" He hunched his shoulders miserably. "Because it's something I've done myself."

Storm widened her eyes, surprised. "You've . . . gotten a dog into trouble? An innocent dog? I don't believe that."

"But I did. You never met Mulch, but he was a dog of the old Pack, and he always hated me. I didn't much like him, either." Lucky huffed a mirthless laugh. "Whine—that nasty little Omega before Sunshine—wanted a promotion, and he wasn't capable of earning it himself. He knew something about me, something terrible, and he forced me to frame Mulch so that Mulch would be demoted. If it had been any other dog . . ." He sighed. "Oh, I confess I'd probably have done it anyway. The fact that it was my enemy made it a little less difficult, that was all. But yes, I stole prey and made sure that Mulch was blamed for it. It was deliberate and cruel, and I lied to my Alpha."

"The last Alpha?" Storm was shocked. "The half wolf? How did you dare?"

"Yes, *that* Alpha. And I was terrified, but I had no choice. I needed to protect the Leashed Dogs, and I didn't want to die, killed by Alpha for being a spy . . . so I had Mulch severely punished instead. And he was innocent, Storm, as innocent as Moon undoubtedly is. So, yes, this situation bothers me far more than

I'd like. To think another dog would be as conniving and dishonest as I was . . ."

Lucky raised his head, and she saw that his face was full of deep shame.

Storm lashed her jaws with her tongue. She had no idea what to say. The story was dreadful; no wonder her Beta wasn't proud of himself. Indeed, she thought as her head whirled, she couldn't even imagine Lucky doing such a thing. He'd done exactly what some dog had just done to Moon; yet now he'd gone along with the punishment meted out to the equally innocent Moon. Storm shook her head violently, unable to reconcile his story with the brave and kind Lucky she knew. She opened her mouth to speak, but closed her jaws again with a snap. *There's nothing I can say to this.*

Lucky gave a low whine, hanging his head as if some invisible giantfur paw was crushing it down. "I don't blame you for being disappointed in me, Storm. I'm disappointed in myself, every day."

Storm cleared her throat and jerked up her head. "I didn't know Mulch, Lucky, you're right. But I do know *you*. You've just told me you had to do this, you didn't have a choice. And I believe that! You wouldn't have done it if you hadn't been forced to. I know that as surely as I know the Sun-Dog will run across the sky tomorrow."

"It's true," said Lucky, "but that doesn't excuse what I did. Nothing excuses it."

"I think it does," she insisted passionately. *I won't believe Lucky could do something so terrible of his own free will. I refuse to believe it!* "You had no choice, but whoever did that to Moon? They had a choice. They weren't forced to do this to her, they did it because they wanted to!"

Lucky gave an exhausted nod. "I think that's true, too. But Alpha and I had no option about punishing her. This Pack's been through so much, just to come together. We don't want it to fall apart now."

"I understand." Storm had to say it through gritted jaws, but it was true. She did understand. Her Alpha and Beta could not have done anything else.

"Go back to your den, Storm." Lucky sounded weary and defeated. "Get some sleep; I'm sure you need it. And so do I, believe me."

As she trod after him, back into the camp, Storm's mind was in turmoil, as if rabbits were running around inside her skull. She could see everything from Lucky's point of view: the terrible decision he'd had to support today, and the awful thing he'd had to do to Mulch, just to survive and to protect his friends.

But it didn't help. Her gut still churned with a desperate, frustrated anger, and the long talk with her Beta had done nothing to calm her.

Her tiredness must have gone deep, Storm realized as she blinked her eyes open to beams of light from the Sun-Dog. Her limbs still ached with it as she staggered to her paws, blinking. She felt as if she'd slept for only the briefest of moments.

Stretching, she eased her way into the clearing. Alpha was padding in a determined circle around the perimeter, her elegant head hanging down and her ears drooping. But though she looked exhausted, Alpha marched on doggedly, one paw after another.

"Alpha." Storm trotted to her side. "Is everything all right?"

The swift-dog looked distracted. "Just making sure my legs don't get stiff. These days I seem to spend so much of my time lying down," she complained. "And I need to stay strong, for my pups as well as for the Pack. I have to be as fit as I can be, just in case . . ."

Just in case what? wondered Storm, but at that moment her attention was drawn by a slight commotion on the sunup edge of the glade. Moon was stalking out of the camp, her head held high with dignity as she passed among the dogs of Twitch's Pack. She was heading, Storm realized with an aching heart, for the cliffs and her High Watch.

Ignoring the growls and mockery of Twitch's Pack, Moon paced on, her focus fixed straight ahead. Even when Chase snapped at her tail and barked a laugh, she didn't react. After a heartbeat or two, she leaped up a small outcrop, walked around a shoulder of rock and disappeared from sight.

Ears pinned back, Storm gave a low whine. "Alpha, did you really have to put Moon on High Watch? Those dogs are loving her humiliation."

"It's not just a punishment," Alpha told her calmly. "It's the only way to keep the Pack safe and united. I thought Beta explained this to you."

"He did, but I feel so sorry for her. She didn't steal that food!"

"But the evidence says she did. And unless she is removed from the Pack for a while, the dogs who believe it would grow angrier and angrier. It would split the Pack. Quarrels would become fights, and fights might become all-out war. We don't want another Storm of Dogs right here in our own Pack, do we?"

"No," admitted Storm with a heavy sigh.

"Besides," added Alpha in a kindlier tone, "I *do* want Moon to keep an eye on the longpaw town. From high up she can see any movement there, and I do not want our Pack to be taken by surprise again. If longpaws come our way, I want to know about it—and as soon as possible. Now, you must have duties, Storm. And I will go on walking for a while."

It was a gentle but firm dismissal, and Storm hung back as Alpha paced on.

I still hate that Moon's being punished for something she didn't do.

All the same, it was clear that Alpha and Lucky had thought very carefully about what they were doing. This was no rash sentence the swift-dog was handing out; she was doing what was best for the Pack, even if Moon had to suffer. Their former half-wolf Alpha would have punished Moon far more harshly—swiftly and without a thought and the idea of justice would never have crossed his cold mind.

At least Sweet is a more thoughtful and even-pawed Alpha than he ever was. . . .

It wasn't a completely comforting thought, but it was a little reassuring. Storm tried to hold on to it as she turned to seek out the other hunt-dogs.

CHAPTER TWELVE

A terrible menace lurked in the gray gloom, and Storm was lost.

The fog was like a living creature, snaking thickly around the trees, oozing into her mouth and nostrils so that she dreaded every breath. Storm could see nothing beyond it, and the horror of what might be hidden made her heart beat cold and slow in her chest. Because there was something there, she knew it. She could no longer tell which direction was sunup, and every tree in the forest was an identical, malevolent monster. She would never find her way home, never.

With the smothering fog around her, she couldn't even smell the beasts that waited among the trees. She knew what they were, though: Fierce Dogs. She could see their shadows looming close, keeping pace. The shape of one was outlined for a moment against the wall of gray; it stopped dead, turning its head toward her. Glowing red eyes pierced the fog, like the bright claws of some Spirit Dog.

And the eyes were coming closer now . . . closer . . . yet the body remained a shadow. As the monster lunged forward, Storm gave a howl of horror and fled.

There was no running from it. More pairs of red glittering eyes blinked open in the gloom, all of them fixed on her. The shadow-dogs' barks and howls echoed and rebounded through the trees as they hunted her down, and however fast she ran, she could not escape them. Were they ahead of her, or behind?

Both?

She swerved to the side, skidding and stumbling and racing on, and slammed into something immoveable. The breath was knocked from her lungs as she crashed to the cold earth—

"Storm . . . Storm . . ."

The sinister voice was calling her name. It knew her, it wanted her, it had her trapped and helpless. Tendrils of fog drifted away as a vast shadow loomed above her, drawing closer. And Storm gave a shrieking whine of terror as she saw its face—

"Storm! STORM!"

The bark snapped her abruptly into wakefulness. Storm reeled on her paws, dizzy and disoriented, but though her paws slithered under her, she didn't fall. The face of the Fierce Dog who stood over her wasn't obscured by fog; it was clear, and concerned, and his eyes were brown, not a glaring, violent red.

"Arrow," she gasped.

He stood among trees that weren't monstrous at all. Pale light from the Sun-Dog's rays gilded their trunks, and their leaves rustled as the Wind-Dogs romped playfully with the Forest-Dog.

"Storm, are you all right?" Arrow ducked his head a little, to make her meet his eyes. "I saw you wandering out of camp."

She shook her whole body, trying to rid herself of the last traces of the dream. "I'm fine, Arrow. Fine. I shouldn't have gone for a walk, I was tired already. I guess I fell asleep out here." She began to shoulder her way past him.

He stepped sideways, blocking her way. "That's not true, Storm. When I saw you walk out of the clearing, it was like you were asleep already. You nearly stepped on Chase! And when you got to the trees, you kept bumping into them."

"I was just—tired, I—"

"You were walking in your sleep, Storm." His gruff voice was anxious. "How long has this been happening?"

Storm's legs felt suddenly too weak to hold her. Slumping against the closest tree trunk, she closed her eyes and tried to breathe deeply.

"I don't know," she muttered. "Since the Storm of Dogs, I think? Since I battled Blade. But the truth is, Arrow, I really have no idea. I could have been doing it my whole life and I might just never have known."

Arrow cocked one ear, twisted his muzzle thoughtfully, then padded over to sit on his haunches beside her. "Why does this wandering bother you, Storm? Lots of dogs do odd things in their sleep; I've seen sleeping dogs chase rabbits. Their legs race, yet they're still lying flat on the ground! Are you worried there's something wrong with you? That you're strange and different?"

"I am not different!" But she was too tired for her snap to carry any true defiance.

"Listen, if that's what you're worried about, you're not alone."

She slanted her eyes at him. "What does that mean? Have you had dreams that made you lose control?"

Arrow hunched his sleek shoulders. "No," he said, "but I know how it feels to be a stranger-dog within a Pack. I know how it feels to be a Fierce Dog among . . . well, non-Fierce Dogs. When I saw Ripper's body in that longpaw town . . . it just came home to my own den, how different I am."

Storm felt confused. "You liked Ripper a lot?" She tried to imagine Arrow and Ripper in a fond, loving relationship, but it was too weird a concept. *What use would Fierce Dogs have for such nonsense, anyway?*

"No," admitted Arrow. "To be honest, I didn't like Ripper much at all. I won't miss her, but when I saw her lying there, dead . . . Oh, I can't put my paw on it. She was just lying there, half of her gone to the Earth-Dog already, and the rest on the way. She wasn't a Fierce Dog, she was a Nothing Dog. She didn't exist anymore, she wasn't a danger, she was gone altogether."

"Uh," mumbled Storm. "That happens to all dogs in the end. It's how Earth-Dog and the Sky-Dogs have arranged the world."

"Maybe, but I was born in the Dog-Garden and brought up in Blade's Pack. I was always told Fierce Dogs were invincible, that nothing and no dog could harm us. We were the commanders of everything around us. It doesn't matter if Ripper was bad, or even if she was good and I never knew it. None of that matters in the end. It all finished with her lifeless on the edge of that hardstone." He shook his head in bewilderment. "A Fierce Dog, dead and helpless. That was hard for me to see. Harder to believe."

Storm swallowed, studying him. She'd never heard Arrow say so much, and she'd certainly never known that such deep thoughts occupied his head. "Why are you telling me this?"

He sighed. "I don't know. Because you look so unhappy? I want to make sure you know you're not strange, or odd, or even *wrong* somehow."

"We are different. You can't deny that, Arrow."

"Yes, in some ways." Arrow's ears twitched forward, and his

voice softened. "But no dog in this Pack will ever understand what it means to be a Fierce Dog. To have all this strength and power, and yet have to hold it down, all the time! That control needs another kind of strength, doesn't it? If the others knew what a struggle you face, and how well you succeed, they'd respect you a lot more."

Storm blinked in surprise. "Thanks, Arrow."

A surge of gratitude warmed her rib cage. She wouldn't admit it to Arrow, but it did feel good to know she had an ally who understood her, just a little. It made more of a difference than she'd thought, having another Fierce Dog in the Pack. Maybe he was more family than she'd realized.

Arrow scratched his ear with a hindclaw, then rose to his four paws. "Let's keep all this between us, shall we? I don't want any other dog to know how I felt when I saw Ripper."

"Of course." Storm nodded solemnly. "I understand."

"Good. If they think it upset me, they might assume I'm still loyal to Blade. And how stupid is that? I made my choice; I turned my back on Blade's Pack. And even if I hadn't, I can't be loyal to a dead dog." He shrugged. "I'll see you back at camp, Storm. Don't be long, and don't do any more walking—you'll need all your energy for hunting!"

With that he trotted off into the trees, a sleek black-and-tan shadow. Storm watched him go, a little bemused. *Why didn't he stay to walk back with me?*

She sighed. She supposed he couldn't help being a bit of a loner within their Pack. Setting off back toward the camp herself, she picked over her dream again in her head.

Maybe I should tell Lucky the truth. Tell him the details of these dreams, and how they make me walk in my sleep. He was a Lone Dog, and he's met many dogs on his travels. He might have met one with the same problem as me. He might know what to do. . . .

Wrapped in her thoughts, she was absent-mindedly following Arrow's scent back to the glade, so when it veered off into the forest, it took Storm a moment to realize she was going astray. Surprised, she halted.

Storm sniffed the still air. Should she follow him, or go back alone to the clearing? Doubtfully, she took a few more steps in his trail, and that was when she heard the voices.

Arrow's gruff tone was instantly recognizable. Storm cocked an ear, uncertain. He was talking to another dog, then; but this one was unmistakably female.

A sudden bark of laughter from Arrow made her jump. Then he murmured more words she couldn't hear, and the unseen female dog made a reply filled with amusement.

Hairs prickled on the back of Storm's neck, and her blood ran cold. *What are Arrow and this dog up to? Why would they meet in secret? Are they plotting against the Pack?*

Not long ago she wouldn't have believed it, but now—who knew? As the tensions within the Pack had grown in the last few days, Storm reckoned, so had the likelihood of mischief. Arrow had sounded so disconsolate about Ripper's death; had it affected him so much that he had decided to betray the Pack—the dogs who had never tried to understand his Fierce Dog nature? He could be bluffing about his detachment from Blade's old Pack. Some of them might still be in the forest, biding their time.

I have to find out. I can't just go back to the camp, and wonder. I have enough trouble sleeping as it is!

Beneath her paws was the soft mulch of rotting leaves, the damp detritus of a whole long Ice Wind. Making her decision, Storm lay down and rolled thoroughly, coating her head and flanks and rump in the odors of the forest floor. When she clambered back to her paws, she rubbed herself briskly against a pine trunk until the sweet, resiny scent clung to her fur.

Taking a deep breath, she crept toward the murmuring voices. Surely she'd masked her own scent well enough by now to fool even Arrow's keen nostrils?

He joked about me wasting all my energy, walking in my sleep. Grimly, Storm clenched her jaws. *If I catch him plotting with our enemies, he'll find out just how much energy I have left!*

On she crept, placing her paws with care, avoiding every twig and dry leaf. She slunk between the trees and through the underbrush like a weasel, sinuous and silent. Arrow's voice was clearer now; she could make out every word he growled. And she recognized that other, female voice now.

Storm froze on the edge of a branch-littered dip in the ground. A massive sycamore trunk rose up in front of her, so ancient that some of its thick and twisted roots snaked up out of the ground. Between those roots, the two dogs were nestled together, heads on each other's flanks. One coat was black and sleek and shining; the other rough, shaggy, and golden.

Bella!

Storm's jaw sagged open. Lucky's litter-sister was the Fierce Dog's secret mate?

I should have known, she realized. *I saw them out in the woods together, when they had no reason to be!*

Then it struck her like Lightning's paw: *That's what Bella was talking about. How Fierce Dogs had to show they could be trusted, how I shouldn't give the Pack any reason to be hostile to them.*

She wasn't worried about me at all. She was concerned for Arrow!

A ripple of discomfort ran through Storm's fur as she watched Arrow lick Bella's ear. The golden dog gave a lazy, contented sigh. Arrow's tongue moved to wash more parts of Bella's face: her eyes, her jaw, the corner of her mouth. His touch looked so gentle and so affectionate . . . and it embarrassed Storm to her core. She wanted to turn away.

And yet she couldn't, because she was fascinated as well as disturbed. *How can they lie so close to each other? Aren't they hot? Isn't it uncomfortable? Her hipbone's sticking right in his ribs and, ew! How can she enjoy him licking her eyelids like that?*

Storm shuddered. The worst of it was, they were completely wrapped up in each other. Why, she might have been an enemy stalking them, but they hadn't even noticed her! And they weren't so much as glancing around for prey! How was this supposed to help the Pack?

What an unbelievable waste of time, she thought with an inward nibble of disgust.

"Aren't you worried about all this?"

For a horrible instant, Storm thought Arrow had seen her, and she made to pull back into the scrub. Then she realized, with a roll of her eyes, that of course he hadn't. He was still stupidly unaware of his surroundings. The Not-So-Fierce Dog was talking to Bella.

"What if Alpha finds out?" he murmured to the golden-furred dog. "Or maybe worse, what if Beta does?"

"I'm not worried," growled Bella softly. "Lucky will understand. He adapts to any situation, my litter-brother, and he always thinks the best of any dog. I'm more worried about you, Arrow."

"Me? You don't need to worry about me." There was amusement in his tone.

"But the way the other dogs treat you—I *know* it's getting to you. I don't want you to be unhappy. I hate it when they turn their rumps on you."

"Honestly, Bella, I'm not that bothered." He nuzzled her fondly. "Maybe I should worry more, but who cares about them? I don't care what they think or what they say. Not when I'm this happy."

Backing away as quietly as she could, Storm turned and crept back in the direction of the camp.

I'm glad I'm about to go on a hunting patrol, she thought disgustedly. *I need to think about something, to take my mind off that soggy, pup-faced pair . . .*

Better that than the alternative, though. Arrow wasn't a

traitor, and neither was his companion. *I'm glad he's not. I don't think I could have borne it.*

Even a sickly load of romantic rabbit fluff was better than that scenario.

Storm shook herself as she trotted toward the glade, and gave a sniff of disdain—but as she did so, her eyes widened and she inhaled harder. Flaring her nostrils, lifting her muzzle, she searched the air for a further trace of the scent that had snagged on them.

Through the trees she could make out Pack members going about their business: Sunshine gathering extra moss for Alpha's bedding; Snap summoning her hunters; Mickey chatting quietly with Twitch. Clearly they'd noticed nothing unusual, but Storm was sure she'd smelled something wrong. Holding herself still, she moved her head, seeking the elusive tang once more . . . sharp, smoky, and a little sour . . . *Foxes!*

Storm's whole body tensed, her muscles bunching. She'd never seen a fox up close, and for good reason—they didn't dare to come close to the Pack's camp. The dogs outnumbered every fox pack in the forest, and they were so much stronger. So if foxes really had approached the glade, they must be doing it deliberately.

And they must have a plan.

For long heartbeats, Storm hesitated, her blood pounding through her as she glanced back to the place where she'd seen Arrow and Bella. Perhaps she should double back and fetch them? They were two of the strongest, best fighters in the Pack.

But if Storm did that, Arrow and Bella would realize she'd seen them. And it had been pretty clear that they didn't want any other dog to know they liked to cuddle up between the roots of trees.

Anyway, Storm told herself, the fox-scent might be old. There was no point in making a fuss and causing havoc if the foxes had been gone for six journeys of the Sun-Dog. Before she raised the alarm, she'd better check it out for herself.

Licking her chops, she made her decision. Storm turned on her haunches and padded swiftly back into the forest, her nostrils seeking out the clinging trail of fox-odor on twigs and leaves and undergrowth. The farther she stalked, the stronger the smell became, until Storm began to feel a nervous pulsing in her neck. What if she blundered right into the foxes? She was sure she could take them on and beat them, but she would risk injury from sneaky bites and filthy, tearing claws. And that would stop her from hunting for a few journeys of the Sun-Dog.

Storm clenched her fangs and drew back her upper lip. It was tempting to charge on. The rankness of fox was so powerful now, it gave her an almost sick feeling in her belly.

Except that there's a new smell. Storm jerked her head up, startled.

Her nostrils flared, and she let her tongue taste the air. *I'm right. That's not a normal fox-smell.* . . . It was sharp, and rich, and it tasted like metal inside her soft mouth—

Blood!

Storm bounded forward as dread bit at her guts. The blood-stench filled her whole head now, so strong it seemed to pulse behind her eyes. Horrified, she skidded to a halt in a disturbed patch of mud and leaves.

Tattered branches half-covered the ground, but what lay beneath them was still visible. A scrap of reddish-gray fur; the darker, wetter red of blood. Tense with nerves, Storm stepped forward on trembling paws, and sniffed. She pulled back the scrubby undergrowth with her claws, and what she saw made her jump back.

A fox-pup lay sprawled in the dirt. Its tiny teeth were bared permanently in a terrified snarl. Its eyes were wide open, but dull, and flies crawled at their corners. The blood that matted its belly fur was darkening, drying to black at the edges of . . .

Bites.

Storm stared at the little corpse, her heart wrenching inside her with horror. She wasn't fond of foxes, but this one was so small, it could never have posed a threat. Not, at least, to a dog as big as the one that had killed it. Because Storm had seen enough wounds to know for sure that this had been done by a dog.

But why? She licked her chops and shook her head. Dogs did not prey on foxes! Even adult foxes, however pesky and verminous, could be scared away with threats and very little violence. A dog might kill a fox in a battle, like the one back at their old territory that Lucky had told her about, but this was just a pup—and a small one at that.

This pup can't have challenged a dog to a fight. It's not possible!

Which meant just one thing, Storm realized as her stomach churned and her head swam.

This pup's been murdered. By a dog.

The taste in her mouth was horrible now, and Storm found herself drooling to get rid of it. *Not that it will work*, she thought as she backed away, her heart beating hard with a mixture of revulsion and pity. She doubted she'd ever get the sight and smell of the fox pup out of her head.

For a fleeting instant, Storm felt a shuddering wave of relief as the breeze rose and the wind changed, bringing fresh untainted air to her nostrils. But she froze again at once. The air was not fresh at all; or only in comparison to the death-smell of the pup. The rising breeze brought back the reek of foxes. *Living foxes . . . angry foxes . . . and they're coming this way, fast.*

They were heading straight toward the Pack.

CHAPTER THIRTEEN

Storm's breath rasped in her throat as she raced through the woods, leaping fallen branches, dodging looming trunks. She couldn't hear the foxes in pursuit, but then she could hear nothing but the thud and crash of her paws and the pounding of blood in her ears.

As she burst into the clearing and slithered to a halt, she could hear their voices clearly behind her, yelping and shrieking in their high-pitched, nasal barks.

"Killer-dogs, fiend-dogs!"

"Slay helpless cubs, they do. Savages!"

"Evil dogs will pay, yes. Pay! Pay!"

"Suffer! *Then* pay!"

The Pack must have heard the racket of fox yelps already, because they were clustered in the clearing, ears and tails high, eyes full of alarm. Chase yelped a warning; Woody stiffened into

165

his stalk-and-pounce position. Sunshine, interrupted midway through renewing the Pack's bedding, whined nervously through a mouthful of moss and leaves. Thorn and Beetle squeezed and scrabbled out from their den's narrow entrance, fangs bared.

"What's happening, Storm?" snarled Chase.

"Foxes!" Storm barked urgently. Their Alpha was too heavy with pups to fight, and she must be protected. But their Beta—"Where's Lucky? *Lucky!*"

Every dog turned to their golden-furred Beta as he emerged from the den he shared with Alpha. His ears were pricked with shock, his bushy tail stiff and trembling, and his lips were pulled back from his teeth, but he didn't advance. He stood foursquare in front of his den, and he showed no sign of moving. He didn't even bark an order, just stared around the Pack as if he expected them to organize themselves.

Fear and frustration almost choked Storm. This was just like when the loudbirds had come. Lucky was watching over no one but Alpha. *What is he doing? He's in command of these dogs while Alpha can't be! His own mate isn't the only dog he needs to defend!*

"Beta!" yelped Storm desperately. "What do you want us to do?"

"I—" Lucky glanced anxiously back at his den, then spun around as the crash of the foxes in the undergrowth came closer.

"Beta." The resounding growl came from behind him, and every dog started. Alpha was emerging from their den, ponderous with the weight of her belly, but determined. "Don't just stand there. It's you who must give the battle orders. The Pack needs you!"

Lucky blinked, and seemed to snap out of his funk at last. "Of course, Alpha." His face turned grim.

Alpha faced the rest of the Pack. Her eyes looked tired, but they still held a steely glint. "Hold your nerve, and keep your discipline, and we'll withstand these invaders. But Beta, you *must* organize the defense!"

"Yes, Alpha." Lucky leaped forward, barking his commands. "Form a line! Chase, Woody, Snap, Spring: Hold the center. Mickey and Dart, take the sunup end of the ranks. Ruff, Rake, Bruno: reinforce the other end. The rest of you, in between! The most important thing is that you hold the line. Remember!" He turned on his haunches, his eyes finding Storm. "You, Storm—I want you in the very center, between Snap and Woody. You're the strongest dog we have, and one of our best fighters. As for Arrow—"

Lucky came to a shocked halt, even as the Pack raced into the positions he'd given them, shoving and squeezing themselves into a compact defensive force.

"Storm." He bounded to her side, shouldering past Woody. "Where's Arrow?"

Storm glanced fearfully toward the forest, then back at her Beta. "I . . . I don't know."

"How can he vanish at the worst moment?" howled Lucky. Then he shook himself violently. "Never mind, we'll have to manage." He raised his bark again so that it echoed across the clearing. "Pack! Prepare to fight!"

The slap of paws and the smash and crunch of twigs was on the very edge of the glade now, and an instant later the foxes burst through the undergrowth. There were a dozen of them or more, snarling and yipping, their thin muzzles wrinkled with fury. For a few moments all Storm could make out was their enraged eyes, the yellow flash of bared fangs, and a writhing mass of gray fur as they poured across the camp's border. Then she felt a cold and eerie calm descend, and she pulled her own muzzle back in a ferocious snarl as the first fox flew at her. Leaping, she crashed into him in midair and they tumbled to the ground in a growling pile of teeth, fur, and claws.

As she bit, scratched, and thrust savagely at its belly with her hind legs, she saw brief flashes of her Packmates battling. Sturdy

Bruno dodged with surprising agility, clamped his jaws in the neck fur of a fox, and then smashed it to the ground. Snap took the chance to pounce on it, pinning it with her forepaws, but before she could bite, another fox sprang onto her shoulders, clawing at her head and ears. Mickey barreled into the fray, knocking the second fox off Snap.

Storm finally got a firm grip on her own fox's scruff, and twisted sharply, flinging it aside. It bounced off a pine trunk with a shrieking yelp. But before she could finish it off, she heard a frantic, furious bark.

"Get off him!"

Thorn was darting and dashing around a snarling ball of fur and teeth. A fox had Beetle's shoulder clamped between its teeth, and Beetle was squirming and clawing frantically to free himself. Storm saw at once why Thorn was keeping her distance: if she mistimed her attack, she could easily end up wounding her own litter-brother.

And Thorn must remember all too well what happened the last time foxes attacked the Pack—I was told how her smallest litter-brother, Fuzz, was killed. No wonder she's hesitant!

Abandoning her own dazed fox, Storm raced across the

clearing. Thorn looked agonized by indecision; she kept rushing toward the bitter struggle, then backing off, and Storm could hear her terrified whimpers.

"Get off my litter-brother! *Please!*"

Memories of pain and death could badly affect a dog's ability to fight—it was only survival instinct, after all. Thorn was rearing back, raising her paws to strike, then dodging back yet again. *She's afraid for her brother—and for herself. And she's right to be!*

Thorn must have heard the story of Bella's betrayal many times—that awful moment when Lucky's littermate had turned up with foxes to attack the half wolf's Pack. *And where is Bella now? She and Arrow are two of our best fighters, and Breeze isn't here either!*

It didn't matter, not right now. What mattered was getting that fox's teeth out of Beetle's bleeding shoulder. Storm slowed her pace, eyed the writhing Beetle and the snarling fox, then crouched and flew at them from a low angle. Her jaws clamped satisfyingly on the fox's haunch, and it shrieked with shock as she snapped her head back and flung it aside.

Storm had no time to enjoy her success. She left Thorn desperately licking the wounded Beetle, and raced to help Chase as she fought off two of the foxes at once. The glade was a chaos of yelps, shrieking howls, and savage barks, and the crash of bodies as they fell or flung themselves into battle. The racket and the thrash of fighting creatures was so overwhelming, it took Storm longer than it should have to realize that reinforcements had arrived, and that the tide of the skirmish was turning.

There were more dogs here, she realized—Arrow had sprung into the clearing, his brutal fangs bared as he drove three foxes efficiently back into the trees; and Bella too, whose former alliance with foxes didn't seem to dampen her fury now. A white-and-black flash rocketed past Storm's vision and she realized Moon must have hurtled down from her High Watch when she'd heard the commotion. Moon had a bitter grudge against foxes, since the killing of Fuzz, and she didn't hold back as she flew at them.

The foxes were backing off now, heads lowered, still snarling; but the dogs of the Pack were exhausted too. Jaws slavering, breath rasping, the two forces faced each other in ragged lines. There were splatters of blood and torn fur all over the suddenly quiet glade.

One of the foxes shook itself, then bared its fangs in a renewed snarl. "Nasty brutish dogs," it hissed. "Bullies! Savages!"

"A fox calls us savages?" growled Moon through clenched teeth. "That's funny."

Another fox, panting hoarsely, snapped, "Dogs think they own the forest, do they?"

"Oh yes," snarled the leader. "All the prey, yes, all the creatures. Dogs rule, dogs do as they like. Think they kill cubs and nobody dares bite back!"

"We bite back," growled another. "Yes, we does."

"Kill cub-pups for fun?" The leader spoke again, his breathing harsh. His pelt was matted and dirty, and his eyes leaked yellow streaks. "No, we don't let you. Some dog pays for this crime!"

The line of dogs yielded as Alpha pushed through from the rear, walking with dignity and elegance despite her swollen belly. She glared into the fox leader's rage-crazed eyes.

"We know nothing of any dead pup of yours," she told him. "We only know about a pup *your* kind killed." She nodded at Moon, who snarled low in her throat.

"Dog-scents in our camp, oh yes," he growled. "Explain that, hm? Can you? No! And just before cub went missing. Dogs killed him!"

"No," said Alpha, a dangerous edge to her tone. "Dogs did not!"

The fox yowled with anger. "Yes! Cub-pup's body is near here! Almost in dogs' camp! *Dogs killed!*"

Alpha drew herself up and took another pace forward, till her muzzle was close to the fox's. "Leave," she growled calmly. "Leave now, and do not come back."

Moon stepped to her side. "Do as our Alpha said." Her voice was menacingly soft. "Dogs do not kill anyone's pups. Dogs aren't cruel and vicious, not like foxes."

Storm, watching nervously, licked her jaws. *I can't say anything. Not here, not now. But some dog is that cruel and vicious, Moon.*

For a horrible, dragging heartbeat, Storm feared the bristling standoff might erupt into violence again. She knew that Moon still mourned little Fuzz, and the death of her mate Fiery had given her an even fiercer determination to protect her surviving pups, Thorn and Beetle. Her hatred of foxes would be more than enough to make her lunge for the leader's throat. . . .

"You lie," snarled the fox. "Lie and kill. Brute dogs!"

But Moon only gave a coughing bark of contempt. "We don't kill pups," she said. "But that doesn't mean we won't kill grown foxes if they attack us, unprovoked."

The fox leader remained silent as he glared at her with hate. Then he flicked his brush, and turned his rump contemptuously on the dogs. He cast a parting snarl over his shoulder. "Not over, this. No. Over it isn't."

His mob followed as he slunk off into the trees, and soon the foxes had melted into the shadows of the forest. Storm felt a wave of relief, but it was swiftly chased out by dread.

I don't think it's the last we've seen of them.

Alpha turned to the Pack, her expression bewildered and angry. "What caused this? Does any dog know what that was about?"

The Pack shared glances, looking as baffled and nervous as their Alpha. Chase flicked his tail anxiously, shaking his head. Mickey whined in denial. Sunshine crouched at the rear of the ranks, whimpering in confusion. Bruno licked his bloodied jaws, perplexed, and Woody and Ruff growled simultaneously, "No, Alpha."

Storm watched all their eyes, searching desperately for the smallest hint of guilt, but there was nothing. All the dogs of the Pack were here by now, Breeze as well as Arrow and Bella and Moon, but every dog looked like the next, startled and exhausted by the shock of the attack.

Storm whined to draw every dog's attention, and sat on her haunches, her head drooping sadly.

"What is it, Storm?" asked Lucky, cocking an ear toward her.

She sighed. "Follow me. I'll show you."

CHAPTER FOURTEEN

"This is . . . this wasn't a hunt." Alpha stood over the corpse of the fox pup, her eyes filled with horror. "This is an obscenity!"

The rest of the Pack gathered around the pathetic little scrap of fur, their ears laid flat, their eyes wide and aghast. The tiny creature looked smaller than ever, as if the forest was already beginning to grow around it and reclaim its remains. Flies hovered and settled around its blank eyes and the bite wound in its belly.

Daisy crept forward, her expression disbelieving as she sniffed pityingly at the fox pup. "Now we know why they were so angry," she whined softly.

"This pup wasn't killed as prey." Lucky's growl was shaky with fury, and he backed protectively against Alpha, as if thinking of his own vulnerable pups in her belly. "There was no reason at all."

"It's just been abandoned here!" Mickey's eyes were bright with anger.

"And so close to our camp," growled Dart.

Woody shook his matted head. "I don't understand. I don't believe any of our Pack would do this."

"Wouldn't they?" Breeze curled her muzzle. "I know one kind of dog who'd do it without thinking. And we have two of them in our Pack!"

Storm took a breath of surprise as every dog in the Pack turned, some guiltily and some with accusation in their eyes, to look at her. She almost opened her jaws to bark a fierce denial, but their gazes had already shifted. The focus of every dog in the Pack was fixed on Arrow.

"We know Storm too well to think she'd do this," said Dart gruffly. "She grew up in our Pack."

"Arrow didn't," grunted Bruno.

Arrow froze in disbelief, his tail tapping nervously, but before he could gather himself to respond, Breeze barked again.

"You turned up very late for the fight, Arrow. Where *were* you?"

Bella sprang forward, her ears flattened. "This fox-pup has

been dead since before Sun-Dog woke," she barked. "Any dog with a nose can smell that!"

Whisper shifted uneasily. "It doesn't have to be one of the Fierce Dogs at all," he said, shooting a plaintive glance at Storm, who winced. "You were late too, Bella. Maybe you should explain where *you* were."

Bella gave an angry yelp of astonishment. "I had nothing to do with this!"

"I agree," growled Snap, her eyes narrowed. "Bella's not the type to kill foxes. She's more likely to sneak them into the camp as allies. Remember?"

Bella turned on her, shoving her muzzle close to the tan-and-white female. She pulled back her lips to show her fangs. "I made a mistake. And I've *learned from it.*"

"Have you?" snarled Snap.

"Yes! And I'll always regret what I did."

"That's still not an answer to Whisper's question." Snap did not back off in the face of Bella's fury. "Where were you? What were you up to in the forest, Bella, while we were under attack?"

Storm's gut churned, but she could do nothing but sit there, motionless with indecision. *I could tell the Pack exactly what Bella was up* to. *And Arrow, for that matter! But I don't think either of them would appreci-ate the intervention. . . .* She didn't dare even catch Bella's eye, in case her expression gave all three of them away.

I saw something I wasn't meant to see . . . and there's no way I can say it aloud.

"Well, Bella?" Snap cocked an ear mockingly. "We're waiting for an explanation."

"All of you, be quiet!" Lucky's bark was uncharacteristically sharp. His ribs heaved with annoyance, and his face was as thun-derous as the clouds when the Sky-Dogs battled. He pressed even closer to Alpha's swollen flank, and Storm realized he was physi-cally supporting her. The swift-dog was swaying slightly, her legs unsteady, and her eyelids were drooping with exhaustion. *It's the shock and stress from the attack*, thought Storm guiltily, *and this quarrel isn't helping.*

"We have to find out—" began Chase, but Lucky interrupted him with a howl of rage.

"I said, *be quiet!*"

Every dog flinched, pulling themselves closer to the ground and ducking their tails. Storm had never heard their easygoing Beta sound so angry, and it gave her a horrible twist of unease in her belly.

"You're picking fights with one another when your Alpha is about to give birth to her first pups. Have you no respect?" Lucky glared around the Pack, meeting their sheepish eyes. "Are you irresponsible milk-pups yourselves? If you think you can do as you like, because Alpha isn't capable—for now—of biting your sorry rumps, you'd better think about what you'll do when she's back on her paws. Because her teeth are going to be finding a few of your haunches. And in the meantime, I'll take pleasure in doing the job myself!"

No dog dared speak.

"Storm," he snarled. "Take Thorn and Beetle with you, and bury this pup. Give it to the Earth-Dog. I think I can trust you three, more than any grown dog here, to do it with dignity." He swept his cold stare around the Pack again. "We will find out which dog has done this—make no mistake about that. But in the meantime, your Alpha needs to rest, and not one of you has anything to offer but empty accusations. *No dog* is to come to Alpha with this petty bickering anymore. You'll come to me, and I'll decide what problems Alpha needs to hear. Do I make myself clear?"

"But, Lucky . . ." began Bruno.

"You'll call me Beta!"

Bruno flinched back, shocked.

"Beta." Chase padded hesitantly forward. "The Pack needs Alpha to judge—"

Twitch limped to Lucky's side and stood at his shoulder, facing the Pack. "Beta is right. A Pack is only as secure as its Alpha, and your responsibility right now—all of you—is to support her. If Alpha is safe and comfortable, the Pack will be too. She has bigger things to worry about than your squabbles. So do exactly as your Beta says, and be quiet!"

That, thought Storm with satisfaction, seemed to do the trick. Only a few dogs began to open their muzzles, and they very quickly thought better of it. As the dogs dispersed, Lucky shepherded Alpha gently toward their den, and Storm turned to Beetle and Thorn. Beetle was licking disconsolately at his wound, but his fur was dense and he hadn't been hurt too badly. He limped a little as he followed Storm, but she got the impression that his shoulder wound wasn't as bad as the hurt to his pride.

"Thanks, Storm," said Thorn. "For getting that fox off Beetle before it could hurt him."

"Yes, thank you," her litter-brother added, a little grumpily. "I appreciate it, but you know . . . I had that fox right where I wanted it."

Thorn gave a little mocking snort, but Storm licked his ear kindly. "I'm sure you did, Beetle, but it was no problem, and you're welcome. Now, shall we get on with our job?"

She wanted very badly to leave the subject of her attack on the fox. She didn't want the two young dogs to dwell too long on the image of her jaws—her *Fierce-Dog* jaws—clamped on that fox's spine. . . . Instead, very gently, she picked up the body of the little fox, making sure her teeth didn't pierce its damaged body any more.

The three dogs padded farther into the forest till they'd found a softer patch of earth where the stones weren't so large. Storm laid the fox-pup carefully aside on a bed of pine needles while she, Thorn, and Beetle set to digging a hole with their claws. Their muzzles and paws were caked with soil and mud by the time they'd excavated a respectable grave.

"How come we got this job?" grumbled Beetle as he sat back to catch his breath. "Is it because we're the youngest?"

"No," Storm scolded him lightly. "It's because Lucky trusts us to do it properly."

"Hmph." Beetle licked mud from between his paw pads, while Thorn inspected his shoulder wound. They both seemed almost nonchalant now, thought Storm. When the fox-pup had been found they'd been stiff with horror, but now, during the practical work of giving it to the Earth-Dog, they seemed far more reconciled to the nasty business.

Storm turned quickly to the fox pup. Pondering Lucky's motives for just a moment, she'd realized that trust wasn't really the issue, though giving the dirty work to younger dogs had nothing to do with it either. Lucky had assigned Thorn and Beetle to the work because he knew it would give them something useful to contribute.

What was more, it would teach them about the ways of the Earth-Dog. This small job would show them that death, however sudden and terrible, was still a natural thing. The little fox would go to the Earth-Dog now, and he would nourish the forest and the prey creatures that lived in it, so that in turn his tribe would never go hungry. . . .

Lucky's not the most warlike of dogs, Storm thought, *but he's a smart leader. Thorn and Beetle know a little more about death now, and that means they won't be so afraid of it.*

Glancing back at Beetle and Thorn, though, she felt a twist of resigned sadness in her belly. It was a pity that Thorn and Beetle had to accustom themselves to death at all.

They're such good dogs already. They're kind, thoughtful dogs. There's no darkness in them, I can tell that.

A shiver went through her spine, all the way from neck to tail.

I wish I could say the same about myself. . . .

CHAPTER FIFTEEN

"*I don't believe those foxes are* gone forever," Daisy was yipping as Storm, Beetle, and Thorn returned to the clearing. "I think they'll be back. They said so, didn't they?"

"They still believe one of us killed that pup," Woody replied with a twitch of his ears. "And until we find which dog is responsible, and do something about it, I'm sure they won't leave us alone."

Storm padded across the grass to join them. The late Sun-Dog striped the green grass with deep amber light, and despite New Leaf there was a coolness to the air that reached through her fur to tingle on her skin. There were still traces of Ice Wind's breath, then; it must be reluctant to let go of the land it had gripped in its icy talons for so long.

Or maybe all I can feel is the coldness inside me. Storm's muscles rippled with her shiver.

"What if we meet the foxes in the forest?" Ruff's black ears were laid back tight against her head. It was almost time for Twitch's former Omega to join the next patrol, and she was clearly fretting about the new danger. "And what if they come back in the night, when we're not ready for them?"

"That's all what-if," Sunshine told her sternly. "You don't need to worry, Ruff. The patrol dogs watch the camp by night, and Moon is on special High Watch, you know that. If the foxes do return, the Pack will fight them off." The little dog's eyes were bright with confidence; Storm was impressed. Sunshine must have her own fears, but she'd still found it within her to reassure the higher-ranking Ruff.

Storm didn't want to get involved. She padded over to a patch of grass so that she could lie down by herself, but cocked her ear to listen to the other dogs. Making a show of nibbling burrs from between her paw pads, she watched from the corner of her eye as Lucky and Twitch greeted Alpha outside her den.

"This is serious business," Alpha was telling her deputies in a low growl. "The pointless murder of the fox-pup is bad enough, but there's something far more worrying. Whoever killed it left it near here, to draw the fox-pack deliberately. The killer *wanted* the foxes to believe we were responsible. Who would do such a thing?"

"That's not the only mystery," said Lucky gruffly. "What about that stolen food beside Moon's den? None of us really believe she did it." He looked to Twitch for confirmation, and the three-legged dog nodded solemnly in agreement. "Could there be a connection between the fox-pup and the theft?"

Storm held herself very still, her teeth paused delicately around a burr, straining to listen. She was glad Lucky had brought that up; it was something she desperately wanted to know herself.

"Maybe the fox-pup was another message to Moon," added Lucky, shaking his head in perplexity.

"Or maybe . . ." Alpha dipped her pale muzzle and closed her eyes. "I don't want to believe this, but we have to consider it: Could the fox-pup have been Moon's revenge? Foxes killed her little Fuzz. And Moon must have been angry about being sent to High Watch. What if, on the way there, she—"

"No," growled Lucky firmly. "Moon isn't a bad dog. None of us believe she stole the food; do we really believe she's a murderer? Of a *pup*?"

"No." Far from being annoyed at his contradiction, Alpha sounded relieved. "But if not Moon, then who?"

Twitch scratched his ear thoughtfully with a hindpaw. "Bella, Arrow, Breeze, and Moon were all out of camp," he pointed out.

"They came to the fight late, remember? And Storm was outside too. . . ."

That was finally too much for Storm. She bounded to her feet and trotted over to the three leaders. They turned, startled, at her resentful growl.

"I had nothing to do with it! How could you—"

"Storm, calm down." Lucky took a pace toward her. "You're not being accused of anything. Twitch was only setting out the circumstances, so we can get to the bottom of this."

Mollified, Storm sat back on her haunches and licked her jaws. She felt slightly embarrassed at her outburst now, but she couldn't help pondering aloud. "Why would *any* dog come back to join in the fight if they were the one who set it up?" She growled, deep in her throat. "Maybe some dog wanted to look like a hero."

"There's no way it was Bella," Lucky told them firmly. "She wouldn't put the Pack at risk, not after what happened last time. My litter-sister's learned her lesson, believe me."

"What about Arrow?" Twitch cocked his head.

"Yes," murmured Alpha. "I wish I could be certain of his motives."

"He saved us from Blade's ambush," Storm pointed out defensively.

"True, but has the Pack been very welcoming to him since then?" Alpha gazed at each of them. "Most dogs have made it clear they don't trust him. He could have set up the attack so that he could save the day, and earn their respect."

Storm, Lucky, and Twitch were silent. It did sound horribly convincing, Storm realized, with a sinking sensation in her gut.

"Except," said Lucky at last, "if that was his intention, it didn't work. The Pack trusts him less than ever."

"He wouldn't be so stupid," objected Storm fiercely. "And anyway, Twitch, why are you so keen to blame this on a Fierce Dog? Haven't I proven that we aren't all villains?"

"Don't take it to heart, Storm," he told her gently. "I'm only making suggestions. But it seems to me we've ended up with more questions than answers."

"Indeed." Alpha nodded. "And we can't be absolutely sure that no other dog crept out of camp, either. Let's make sure we treat all dogs as innocent until we have proof of wrongdoing."

"Agreed," said Lucky, and Twitch growled his agreement, too. "In the meantime, I must lead another hunt." His eyes were bright and his tail high with what looked like anticipation. Puzzled, Storm pricked up her ears. Was this more than a normal hunt? What was her Beta up to?

* * *

"This is an important hunt," Lucky told his group of dogs as they gathered at the edge of the clearing. "And not just because we need prey. I want you all—every dog—to get used to working together. We can't pick and choose who we hunt or patrol or fight with, and I want you all to understand that. We have to be able to rely on one another."

Storm studied the other members of the hunting patrol. Bruno was a former Leashed Dog, one of Lucky's original allies. Breeze and Whisper had been in Terror's Pack. Snap had been a longstanding member of Sweet's Pack, since well before Sweet rose to Alpha. And she and Arrow were Fierce Dogs, but only one of them had called Blade their Alpha. Storm understood Lucky's motives in selecting dogs of every Pack, but she couldn't help feeling apprehensive about how it would work out in reality.

As she followed Lucky into the forest and toward the hunting meadows of Twitch's old territory, she became aware that Arrow was keeping close to her shoulder. It was natural, she supposed—Fierce Dog sticking with Fierce Dog—but it seemed to go against Lucky's whole purpose. And it made her irrationally twitchy.

Silly, she thought, *when I've just been defending Arrow to Lucky, Alpha, and Twitch.* All the same, she deliberately veered to the side, trying to detach herself gently from his company. *The other dogs mustn't think Fierce Dogs can only befriend each other!*

Avoiding the company of Arrow, though, only brought her too close to Whisper. His eyes lit up in his gray-furred face as she edged closer to him, and she forced herself to gaze firmly to the front. *Please don't start, Whisper,* she thought. *I don't need another round of hero-worship. . . .*

Storm found herself so wrapped up in avoiding both Arrow and Whisper, she was surprised when Lucky came to a halt. The hunting meadow opened up ahead of them, sunlit and promising, and Lucky licked his jaws, looking satisfied.

"I think we're going to have good hunting today," he told them in a rumbling growl. "There have always been rabbits here. Let's sniff them out. Cautiously, now. We don't want to alarm the prey."

Spreading out as they padded silently into the field, the dogs buried their snouts in the long grass, scenting deeply for hints of small creatures. Storm narrowed her eyes and flared her nostrils. There was definitely something here: a trace of rabbit, certainly, but it was overlaid with something stronger and more recent. Closing her eyes altogether, she let the scent drift deep into her nasal passages.

Her eyes sparked open. "I think there's a deer!"

Arrow turned expectantly. Whisper darted over to her, ahead of the others, his tongue lolling with enthusiasm.

"Really, Storm? Where?"

"Sniff and you might find out." Arrow rolled his eyes and buried his own muzzle in the damp grass.

"You're right, Storm." Lucky's ears were pricked high with anticipation. "I don't think it's the same scent I followed before, but it's definitely a deer."

All of Storm's worries fell away as a buzz of excitement tingled through her blood. "Could it be the Golden Deer?"

"Let's follow the scent and find out." Lucky's eyes brightened, and he trotted off in pursuit of the trail. "Fan out behind me, and make sure I stay on track!"

The dogs did as they were ordered, Storm staying close to Lucky's haunch. The Beta seemed in no danger of losing the trail, and the scents didn't deviate or take any unexpected turns. As the hunt patrol reached the far edge of the meadow, the odor of deer was stronger than ever.

Storm raised her head, her nostrils full of the promise of deer flesh. A thin line of scraggy birches lay in front of them, but there was no thick, dark forest behind them, only more open fields. Beams of sunlight picked out a slender, long-limbed creature browsing the grass beneath the trees.

Every dog went stock-still, nose lifted. Storm could feel her heart pounding her rib cage, and for a moment she was afraid the deer would hear it. The Sun-Dog's fiery light surrounded the grazing creature in a glow of gold, and Storm's breath caught in her throat.

Is it the Golden Deer? I don't detect that special scent, like before, but maybe . . .

Lucky flicked a glance over his shoulder, and dipped his head to the other dogs, but despite his silent caution, the deer's head jerked suddenly up. Storm saw its large ears flicker with alarm as it froze, staring in their direction. Then it spun and bolted, crashing through the undergrowth.

"Go!" With that, Lucky was hurtling after it, his hunters at his heels.

Storm raced after him, her paws flying. The belt of trees was narrow but the deer knew how to use them, doubling back and darting and dodging, slowing down the less-nimble dogs. The others were falling back, despite their baying howls of determination, and even Storm stumbled as she changed direction and almost crashed into a tree trunk.

Lucky, though, was running faster than Storm had ever seen

him. His paws were quick and his body was agile, and he twisted and swerved almost as fast as the deer. In fact, she realized, he was leaving them all behind. Grimly she pounded on, trying to cut across the deer's path at a wider angle, but it burst from the trees and fled across the next expanse of meadow. Lucky was only a rabbit-chase behind it.

Storm raced in pursuit. She could hear the rest of the hunters following her, but she couldn't spare the energy to glance back. The field sloped down at a low angle, and it was covered with yellow-and-white flowers; the deer was so swift its hooves seemed to fly across the lake of blossoms. The creature was still bathed in the pale golden glow that had surrounded it in the trees. It almost made Storm's eyes sting.

She blinked, and the deer had vanished.

No!

There was Lucky, still running hard, and Storm picked up speed to gain on him. The glowing deer was nowhere to be seen, but as they bounded down the steepening slope, they saw something else.

It didn't glow, and it didn't hurt Storm's eyes, but it was undoubtedly another deer. Its pelt was deep russet, and it was grazing contentedly at the farthest border of the meadow.

Lucky slithered to a halt so suddenly, Storm almost tumbled over him.

"Quiet," he growled, crawling forward in the sheltering grass.

Panting as silently as she could, Storm shuffled on her belly till she was alongside him, and together they stared at the unwary creature. A fully grown female, it ripped intently at the grass and flowers. Its ears flicked lazily back and forth, but so far it hadn't spotted them.

The rest of the hunters were behind them now, and luckily they too had noticed the deer in good time. They dropped to crouch low in the grass as they crept forward to their leader. Arrow slunk up to Storm's shoulder, and Snap positioned herself on Lucky's other side.

"What now, Beta?" she growled quietly.

"We'll circle it. Widely and carefully." Lucky's eyes were narrow with concentration as he watched the deer. "Snap, take Whisper and make your way upwind of it, to the sundown side. The rest of us will approach from the other direction. When it runs from your scent, we'll be there to intercept it."

The dogs began to slink into position, placing their paws delicately, keeping heads, ears, and tails low. With Bruno and Arrow to one side and Lucky to the other, Storm eased forward, trying hard not to disturb so much as a blade of grass.

They were so close now, she could hear the rip and crunch of the deer's blunt teeth as it grazed. Storm tried to quiet her excited breaths.

A movement at her side made her turn her head. Bruno was starting to rise, and Arrow too was lifting his paws to pace forward.

No! They'll scare it too soon—

Then she saw a dark brown shape move swiftly between the two dogs to nudge their flanks. *Breeze,* she realized. *Thank the Sky-Dogs. She must have realized they were about to ruin it.* Bruno and Arrow sank back to their careful stalking positions.

Lucky's ears were quivering with alertness now, and the tip of his tail was flicking. He crawled forward again, one pace and then another. They were so close now, Storm's head felt full of deer-scent. Drool gathered at the corners of her jaws.

Abruptly the deer started, its head flying up. But it wasn't looking at them, Storm realized; it had smelled the approach of Snap and Whisper from upwind.

Spinning on its delicate hooves, the deer sprang to flee, but Lucky gave a sharp bark and leaped for its raised throat. Storm and his other hunters were right behind him, and the deer had nowhere to go. Panicking, it tried to jump clear over them, but Arrow's jaws found its hind leg and dragged it down. The dogs pounced, dodging its wildly kicking limbs, and Whisper and Snap joined in, bearing the helpless deer down. In a few short moments, the hunt was over.

The dogs stood over their prey, panting with the sudden exertion, but their eyes glinted with triumph. *We're a team,* Storm realized with a flush of delight. *That worked perfectly, because we worked together.* Snap sat down to lick her haunch; Arrow stared happily at the deer's corpse. Whisper couldn't repress a *wuff* of excitement, and Bruno nodded, licking his chops.

Storm's pleasure faded a little, though, as she stared back at the deer. Its pelt wasn't golden at all, not even in the Sun-Dog's warm light. The short fur that shifted in the breeze was russet-red, flecked with tawny, and scarlet where the deer's throat was stained with blood.

Lucky nudged her questioningly. "What's wrong, Storm? That was good work from us all."

"It's not a Golden Deer." She sighed. "I really thought we had one this time."

"So did I." He licked her ear. "But it doesn't matter. I think there was something special about the first deer, the one we saw in the trees, but this one wasn't it."

"I know. Where did it go? I was so sure we had it."

"Storm, we may not have caught the Golden Deer, but I think the Wind-Dogs were looking after us all the same. Didn't that deer lead us straight to this one? I'm not going to complain, that's for sure." Lucky's tongue lolled with delight and he flicked his ears. "Every dog will have a full belly tonight, even Sunshine and Moon!"

"That's true." Storm felt instantly cheered by the thought that Moon would be able to share in the Pack's luck, despite her ongoing punishment. "Let's get it back to the camp, then."

Rising to her paws, she sank her jaws into the deer's foreleg, but then cocked one ear and hesitated, releasing it.

"Beta. Do you hear that?"

All the dogs were on their paws now, looking nervously at the sky where it met the line of the trees. There was a low humming, which quickly became a clatter, and then a subdued rattling roar. Faint black shapes rose above the horizon.

"Loudbirds!" yelped Whisper.

"We're in the open!" barked Lucky. "Every dog under cover, now!"

"But the deer—" began Snap.

"We can come back for it. Right now we have to hide!" Lucky sprinted for the edge of the meadow as the racket of loudbirds swelled and their shadows grew larger.

There's no time to get back to the trees, Storm realized with a moment's panic. And they would be seen for sure if they crossed beneath the path of the loudbirds. . . .

"There!" barked Snap, and veered to the side, heading for the meadow's corner.

Storm saw at once where she was heading: a large patch of twisted scrub that grew thickly against the edge of the meadow. All the dogs turned to race after Snap, and they plunged one after another into the prickly thicket, cowering down against the earth. It wasn't the best cover, Storm realized—the tangled branches barely came as high as Arrow's ears—but it would have to do.

She strained her eyes upward along with the other dogs, and they watched with their breath in their throats as the loudbirds roared over the meadow. The first great monster turned, swept low, and hovered, its wings a blur. It was so close, Storm could make out the longpaws crouched in its belly.

"Will the loudbirds roost here?" Whisper's hoarse voice trembled.

"Quiet!" snapped Lucky in a growl.

Shamed into silence, Whisper pressed himself closer to Storm. She could feel his muscles trembling against her flank, and she wanted to flinch away, but she had no choice but to lie still. All she could do was clench her jaws and bear it.

"I feel much safer with you here," he whispered.

Bruno, behind Storm, grunted dismissively. "You'll be safe if you don't draw her fangs in your direction."

Her irritation at Whisper's clinginess faded abruptly in the face of Bruno's snide disdain. *I should be furious at that remark*, thought Storm miserably, *but all I am is sad. Does Bruno really think I killed that fox-pup?*

Perhaps they all think that, deep down . . . perhaps some dogs will never trust me at all. She wanted to whimper her misery.

"You'll never hurt me," murmured Whisper, as if he'd overheard her unhappy thoughts. "You don't put the Pack in danger—you protect us!"

"That's nice of you to say, Whisper," Storm muttered, "but—"

"It's *true*," he insisted. "You killed Terror, and freed us from the tyranny of the Fear-Dog! I don't think I'll ever be able to repay you for what you did."

Does he have to go on about it? Storm turned her face away from his adoring eyes. Breeze, on her other side, twitched one ear, but said nothing.

They've all noticed, Storm realized grumpily. *He's getting embarrassing.*

The relief, when the loudbirds rose away from the meadow and their clattering noise faded at last, was overwhelming, and Storm found herself sighing out a huge breath. At last she could squirm away from Whisper and emerge into the clear air, stretching her muscles.

Beside her, Lucky pulled a jagged twig out of his tail fur with his teeth. He shook his fur out vigorously, then turned to them all.

"That was a close one," he said with feeling. "Now let's take turns dragging that deer back to camp. That way no dog will get overtired."

Panting with relief, the dogs of the hunting party followed their leader. Storm felt anticipation rise in her again, along with a more cheerful mood. It would be good to get the enormous prey back to the Pack, and to hear their barks of respect and appreciation.

She bounded to Lucky's side as he came to an abrupt halt. He was staring at the ground, and for a moment Storm couldn't understand the shock in his eyes. Then her heart plummeted.

Snap trotted up beside them. "What happened to the deer?" she whined in confusion.

"I don't understand." Bruno stood behind them, bewildered. All the dogs fell silent as they gathered around Lucky, and they all gazed in disbelief.

Where the carcass had lain, there was now only a patch of flattened grass, and a drying stain of blood.

CHAPTER SIXTEEN

A breeze rustled through the meadow, stirring the grass where the deer had lain, teasing the dogs with its lingering scent. Lucky shook his head slowly.

"What happened to it?" he growled in confusion.

Whisper crept timidly to Storm's side. "Maybe it wasn't really dead?"

"Is that it?" Bruno frowned. "Maybe it got up and ran away while we were hiding."

"No," said Lucky with certainty. "Prey can be clever, but not *that* crafty. A deer couldn't lie there playing dead. It would have panicked long before we abandoned it."

"Some other creature took it, then," said Snap grimly.

"Could it have been the longpaws?" Storm was hesitant even to suggest it, but she could think of nothing else. "Maybe the loudbirds landed and we didn't notice."

"Or they just picked it up in their talons?" Arrow cocked his head, bemused.

"Maybe that's it." Lucky couldn't tear his eyes away from the empty patch where their prize had lain. Storm could almost smell his crushing disappointment.

"I know," suggested Whisper. "The deer must have got up again, like the Golden Deer does every New Leaf. Isn't that what Alpha said they do?"

"I think you might have a point," growled Bruno, and Breeze gave a nod of agreement.

"No," snarled Storm, and every dog turned to look at her in surprise. "That's nonsense, if you ask me. That wasn't a Golden Deer, it was a normal one! Whatever happened here, there's a much more ordinary explanation." She turned to glare at them all, lashing her tail in frustration. "But it doesn't matter, does it? All that matters is that we don't have any prey for the Pack!"

A nagging hunger nipped at Storm's belly, and she turned over where she lay, stretching out her legs and glowering at the walls of her den. Was everyone else having this much trouble sleeping? No dog had eaten well, after all: a few mice, two voles, and a skinny squirrel had made up the entire prey pile this evening.

Her inner question was answered quite unexpectedly when a commotion rose suddenly outside her den. Storm pricked an ear and raised herself up on her forepaws. She could hear angry barks and snarls, and bitter voices of accusation.

Oh, Sky-Dogs help us, she thought irritably. *What is it now?*

Scrambling to her paws, Storm ducked out of her den and stalked toward the knot of quarreling dogs in the center of the clearing. At least, she'd assumed it was a quarrel, but as she drew closer, she could see it was a very one-sided one; Breeze, Bruno, and Dart stood around Arrow, snarling, their hackles bristling. Arrow could only turn warily, eyeing each dog in turn and keeping his jaws shut.

Alpha squirmed from her den as more dogs appeared. The swift-dog's belly looked heavier and rounder than ever, as if her flanks could barely contain the growing pups, and there was exhaustion in her dark eyes. Lucky hurried to her side, then turned to bark to Twitch, who was hobbling closer.

"We've got to do something about this, Twitch. Right now!" Anxious, Lucky nosed Alpha's shoulder, then snarled loudly. "Another trivial problem for Beta and Third Dog to solve, but let's leave Alpha out of it."

Alpha didn't look as if she even had the energy to argue; her expression was all weariness at yet another squabble in the Pack. Without a word she turned and limped back to her den.

Storm felt a pang of pity for her, but she couldn't wait for Lucky and Twitch to try to sort this out with yet more talking; bolting forward to stand in front of Arrow, she turned to face down Breeze, blocking the two dogs from each other with her body.

She curled her muzzle warningly. *I'm defending Arrow*, she thought, *but I hope Breeze realizes it's her I'm protecting. If she gets into a real fight with a Fierce Dog, she won't stand a chance.*

Lucky and Twitch at last managed to nose their way through the crush of dogs. Lucky nipped and snapped at several inquisitive muzzles, then turned ferociously on the instigators of the trouble.

"The Pack's just eaten, and you're fighting? I'm disappointed in you all!" His dark eyes flashed. "This is the time for resting. You'll have to hunt a lot more effectively tomorrow, after tonight's sorry prey pile!"

"But Beta," began Dart, "Arrow's been sneaking around. He's up to something!"

"Quiet!" Lucky's bark was so savage, Dart clamped her jaws together abruptly. "Arrow is part of this Pack, or had you forgotten? He's the one who saved us from Blade's ambush. I wish some of you would remember that, and appreciate him a little more!"

Dart hung her head and ducked her tail, but her expression was resentful. Storm was surprised to find herself sympathizing. *This isn't really about Arrow, not this time. Every dog is on edge, what with loudbirds and longpaws, and waiting for the foxes to attack again at any moment.*

"Every dog, gather round." Lucky stood with his head high, his expression cold and determined.

"I'll fetch Alpha . . ." Storm began, turning, but Lucky gave a short, sharp bark to stop her.

"No, Storm. Alpha needs her rest. I'll report to her later." He padded around the Pack members, some of whom had the grace to look ashamed of themselves. "I've got a suggestion that might help with the tensions around here."

They watched him expectantly. Mickey and Dart glanced with nervous expectation at each other; Daisy lay down, her head tilted up toward Lucky and her dark eyes full of hope. Clearly, thought Storm, she wasn't the only one who'd like to see an end to the damaging squabbles.

Twitch nodded. "Go ahead, Beta. I think the whole Pack is open to ideas."

"I think there needs to be a new role in this Pack. Something between hunt dog and patrol dog; a new rank. I suggest we create a new position: we'll call it *scout dog*."

There was a long silent pause, until Mickey tilted his head. "That sounds . . . interesting."

"What would a scout dog do?" asked Bella curiously.

"The job will need a small, quick dog," Lucky explained. "The task would be to accompany the hunting patrols, specifically to keep an eye out for danger. The scout will keep watch for loudbirds, longpaws, and foxes so that the hunting patrol can concentrate on finding food. And he or she will also stop prey from being stolen from under the hunters' noses," he finished pointedly. "The Pack will have more food, and we'll all feel safer. And then maybe this foolish fighting will stop."

Storm nodded, remembering their crushing disappointment at the loss of the deer. "It does make sense."

"Sounds good to me," growled Bruno.

"And me," added Snap, "but you'll have to choose these scouts, Beta."

"Yes. And I suggest Whisper, and Dart, to begin with." Lucky nodded at them. "You two are fast, and you've got good eyes and noses."

Whisper and Dart exchanged a pleased glance, and their tails thumped the ground.

"And any other dog can volunteer, if you think you're suited for this work," Lucky went on, pricking his ears at the assembled dogs.

Breeze took an immediate pace forward. "I'm fast too, Beta. And I'm a hunter already. I think I'd be helpful in a scouting role."

"Me too." The high excited bark came from Daisy. "I think I'd be good at this, Beta!"

Lucky nodded, and bent down to lick her shaggy white ear. "I think you would, too. All right, it's settled. Our new scout dogs will be Whisper, Dart, Breeze, and Daisy."

Storm sat on her haunches, warmed by a sense of optimism. With new and important roles, some of the more discontented dogs might find themselves much happier, and more fulfilled. Didn't every dog just want to feel valued by the Pack, and important to it? Now that some hunters and patrollers were scouts, it would also give the others more chance to shine in their own positions.

And the busier dogs are, the less time and energy they have to whine and fight, Storm thought to herself. *Lucky's really a smart leader. . . .*

Lucky turned as Alpha padded out of her den again and approached the Pack. The swift-dog nuzzled him. "What's happened, Beta?"

"With your permission, Alpha, we're going to establish a new rank of scout dog. Whisper, Dart, Breeze, and Daisy have agreed to do the work. It's necessary, I think, and it'll benefit the Pack in other ways."

Alpha gazed around the dogs, nodding approvingly. "Good idea, Beta. And what does the rest of the Pack think?"

"I like the idea," barked Mickey.

"It seems positive all around," agreed Bruno gruffly.

"It'll help the Pack a great deal, I think." Woody's tail thumped.

All the dogs were barking their agreement now, and there seemed to be a surge of enthusiasm among the Pack. Storm's heart felt lighter by far than it had earlier in the evening. *This Pack can be fixed—we really can form a team!*

Although the dead fox-pup still hasn't been explained. . . . The thought struck her, kindling her unease once more. *And the foxes are bound to return sometime. . . .*

If the foxes launched a sneak attack, no scout dog would be of help. And yes, from now on scouts could protect the prey the dogs gathered when they hunted—but what *had* happened to today's missing deer? At least if a scout had been watching, they would *know* if the longpaws had taken it, or if something else had.

How could it just vanish like that? Storm shook her head violently, trying to clear the fog of confusion inside it. *Could there be something out there, something malevolent? Something that's actually targeting this Pack?*

If there was something so sinister going on, it could only have one purpose: to weaken the Pack by sowing division and stealing prey. *Is it even possible that this enemy's trying to provoke a war between our Pack and the foxes?*

Storm licked her chops in anxiety. But who would do such a thing? Who would even want to?

Entirely against her will, an image formed in her mind: a snarling muzzle, rigid upright ears, small savage black eyes, long deadly teeth. *A Fierce Dog.* Once again, Storm tried to shake the thought away; the trouble was, it wouldn't go.

It wasn't Arrow, she knew that. She was more sure of him than she was of herself!

But there were other Fierce Dogs out there, somewhere. Just because they'd seen Ripper's dead body, it didn't mean all of Blade's Pack was gone forever. Another dog from that sinister, awful Dog-Garden might be stalking nearby, coming closer, making its devious plans for some end that Storm couldn't guess.

And if she couldn't fathom what they were planning, and why, how could she possibly stop it?

CHAPTER SEVENTEEN

The undergrowth prickled Storm's nose as she pushed through it, scenting for prey. The bushes were still sprouting new leaves, and some of the tiny green thorns that grew with them could be unexpectedly vicious. She winced as one jabbed her mouth, but at her side, Mickey growled encouragingly.

"These thorns would drive a dog mad, I know. Storm, check that fallen tree over there, will you? There might be something living in it."

She spotted the large trunk, which must have fallen a few Ice Winds ago; it was thickly covered in moss and the forest had grown up around it. It did seem like a good prospect for prey, but when she investigated it thoroughly, she discovered nothing more than old traces of shrew.

"There's been a nest of something there, Mickey," she told

him, drawing back, "but they've moved on."

"Don't worry." He sounded disappointed, though. "Woody might find something."

Storm glanced to the side. Despite the thickness of the underbrush, she could make out the brown-and-white dog snuffling around for prey. The hunting party was moving too slowly, she thought with frustration. Now that each hunt patrol included a scout dog, the rest of them could take more time investigating the terrain in detail; but although it might prove more efficient, Storm found the new routine infuriating. When another dog ran ahead to find prey-heavy areas, or to warn them of an approaching threat, Storm herself had no excuse to race across meadows, searching creatures out with her own nose.

I'm sure my legs will stiffen up altogether if we go on like this, she thought dolefully.

She gave a silent sigh, annoyed at herself. Lucky's idea had been a really good one, and she knew it was a more efficient way of hunting. Indeed, she'd been honored and excited to be chosen for the first hunting party to go out with a scout dog. Even when Lucky had assigned Dart to be their scout, Storm hadn't minded. She knew she could handle the skinny chase-dog's snide remarks about Fierce Dogs, so long as Dart did her job properly. But Dart hadn't ended up being their scout after all.

Storm pricked her ears. Ahead of her there was a crashing in the undergrowth, a rustling of leaves and a snapping of twigs, and suddenly Whisper burst into view, his jaw open in a grin as he panted. Storm tried not to wince as his eyes lingered adoringly on hers.

"What's up, Whisper?" she managed to growl.

"Nothing, Storm. All's clear up ahead. No threats that I can smell—and I've smelled all around, for at least two or three rabbit-chases!"

Mickey's throat rumbled disapprovingly. "Whisper, why are you telling this to Storm? I'm the hunt leader today."

Embarrassment drove all the eager cheer from Whisper's features. His ears drooped. "Sorry, Mickey."

"That's all right." Mickey gave Storm a long-suffering glance. "Do get it right next time, though."

"I'll go and check again!" said Whisper, and bolted back the way he'd come.

"Oh, in the name of the Earth-Dog," snarled Storm, when his gray rump had vanished into the undergrowth. "I'm really sorry, Mickey. I wish he wouldn't defer to me all the time. He *knows* I'm not in charge of this hunt."

Mickey gave a growling laugh. "It's not your fault, Storm."

"But I don't know what's *wrong* with him! I wish he hadn't volunteered to be a scout today. Why couldn't he just let Dart do it?" Dart had been all too quick to agree to the swap, and now here was Storm, stuck on yet another hunt with the dog who wouldn't leave her alone.

"I think it's obvious why he couldn't leave Dart to it," growled Mickey, but she could hear the amusement in his voice.

"What?" Storm snapped her head around to stare at him. "What's obvious? I wish you'd explain it to *me*."

"Nothing. Not my place to point it out." But the Farm Dog was still repressing his mirth, she could tell.

"Mickey, what do you mean?" Exasperated, Storm halted.

"Oh, Storm." Sighing, Mickey grew more serious. "Don't you see it yourself?"

"See what? I don't—"

"Whisper's feelings for you might be . . . well, they might be more than normal affection for a Packmate. Do you understand?"

"Not really. I—*oh*." It hit her like a falling branch. She sat back abruptly on her haunches. "No. No, Mickey, that can't be it!"

"I think you'll find it is, Storm. Every dog can see how he looks at you."

215

"Whisper wants to be my *mate?*" Her jaw sagged with horror. "I don't want a mate! *At all!* Especially not Whisper!"

"Oh come on, Storm, you must have thought about having a mate at some point." Mickey twitched his whiskers in surprise.

"I can't think of anything I want less!" she exploded. "Why does a hunter need a mate? What's the point? And . . . *Whisper!*"

"All right, all right." The laughter was back in Mickey's voice. "But I still think it explains his, um . . . affection."

There was a sinking sensation in Storm's gut as she got back to her paws. Mickey was only trying to explain—trying to be kind—but now she felt worse. What was Whisper *thinking?*

At that moment her unwanted admirer returned, panting, through the bushes. Whisper gazed at her, tail wagging happily, but he managed to turn to Mickey before he spoke.

"There's a strong prey smell up ahead, Mickey. In a part of the wood near Twitch's old territory."

Mickey nodded. "All right. This area's not proving very fruitful, so we may as well move on. Well done, Whisper."

The gray dog almost glowed, and he darted his eyes at Storm, as if making sure that she'd heard the hunt leader's praise. "Thanks, Mickey!"

"Woody!" Mickey turned to give a sharp bark, and the thickset dog came bounding over. "Whisper says there's prey ahead—you and I will check it out. Let's go."

Before Storm could protest, the two of them had sprung ahead and disappeared into the undergrowth, and her yowl of desperate appeal stuck in her throat. *They've left me alone with Whisper! Mickey, how could you?*

She could run away, she thought dismally, and try to catch up with Mickey—but Whisper was a fast dog. Why else had he been picked to be a scout? She'd never outrun him. Storm heaved a sigh. *I'm stuck with him till we get to the new prey territory.*

She let her tongue loll, and forced herself to sound upbeat but casual. "Come on then. We should go after them."

Whisper showed no sign of moving. He cocked his head and stared at her, his eyes full of affectionate concern. Storm felt like disemboweling him on the spot.

"Storm, are you all right? After last night?"

Her jaw opened, then closed again. "What? You mean, after the big argument? That was nothing to do with me."

"No, no!" He panted encouragingly and tilted his head. "I mean later, when you walked in your sleep. You didn't hurt yourself, did you?"

Storm's head reeled. She felt as if she'd fallen off a high cliff, and hadn't hit the ground yet. She blinked at Whisper, aghast. At last she managed to draw breath and stammer, "I—I did what?"

"Walked in your sleep. I saw you!"

"No." She shook herself vigorously and tried to push past the gray dog, as panic rose in her chest. "You were dreaming, Whisper."

"I wasn't!" He hurried alongside her as she paced after Mickey. "I was worried, and I waited up, and I saw you come back to the hunters' den. And you were walking, but you were kind of stumbling. You were obviously fast asleep! Storm, I'm worried about you!"

Her mind whirled. Storm felt sick, and there was a lump of dread in her stomach. Whisper clearly had no idea how bad this might be; he was only worried about her safety. "It's nothing, Whisper! Just a bad habit."

"But you could have walked off a cliff, or anything." He pushed in front of her, forcing her to stop.

Storm wanted to sink her teeth in his scruff and fling him out of her way. Instead she gritted her fangs hard. "I said it's nothing! Leave me alone!" *What might I have done*, she thought with sudden horror. *And would I remember doing it? I could have done anything and I'd have no memory of it!*

And why did Whisper, of all dogs, have to see me like that?

"Storm, you can talk to me! Honestly, don't worry. It's no big deal."

"I don't know how you can even say that!" she barked in his face. "I asked you to forget it and leave me alone, so *do that*. Please!"

She barged past him, to find the brush opened out just ahead into a desolate wasteland littered with dead trees and fallen branches. Taking a deep breath, Storm trotted on as fast as she could, but as she'd feared, there was no losing Whisper. He bounded alongside her for a rabbit-chase or more, then at last ran ahead, casting her one final worried glance.

She ignored it, turning her head away with the pretense of searching for Mickey. All she wanted to do was hunt—why did the dogs of her Pack have to make that so difficult? *Why can't they do as I ask, and leave me be? I don't want to think about what Mickey said, and I don't want to think about Whisper, and I certainly don't want to think about my stupid dreams, and the way I seem to act them out. . . .*

"Storm!" Mickey's voice cut into her agonized thoughts. "There's a rabbit trail over by that rotten stump—can you follow it, please?"

I'll do better than that, she thought grimly as she bounded away across the litter of white branches in the direction he'd shown her. *I need to catch some prey. I need to stop thinking!*

The scent trail was easy enough to pick up, but it wound away across the wrecked stretch of land, and Storm found herself entirely uninterested in traipsing after it. Her eyes were younger and better than Mickey's, and she knew what that smear of shadow was beyond the silvered trunks of dead trees. *A warren entrance!*

Storm swallowed down all her anxieties and frustrations, and sprinted over to the burrow. Plunging her muzzle in, she breathed deeply. *Yes! There's a rabbit in there!*

She needed no further incentive. Letting excitement sweep through her muscles and veins in a great tide, she hurled herself at the burrow. She dug ferociously, thrusting her claws in, dragging up the earth till it showered around her and her chest and shoulders were spattered with soil.

Still she dug, tearing at the ground, her muscles working furiously. The scent of the rabbit was almost overpowering now, and there was more—there was the reek of its fear as she dug closer. It made Storm heady with desire. Her mouth and nostrils were full of soil and her muzzle must be filthy, and mud was clumped between her paw pads, but she didn't care. *So close!*

One last yank with her forepaws, and a huge lump of earth came loose and crumbled. With a yelp, Storm shoved her head and shoulders deep into the burrow, snapping wildly. And sure enough, her jaws closed around soft fur and warm flesh. The rabbit was kicking, flailing desperately as it struggled to burrow deeper, but it was too late. Storm's teeth crunched on its spine. She felt it go limp in her mouth, and she backed out swiftly, the rabbit clenched in her fangs. Storm flung it down and slammed her forepaws onto it.

It was dead, of course. She should feel satisfied, now—so why was she still so angry? Snarling, she seized its haunch in her jaws and tore, feeling the limb come away. *So easy, so weak.* She bit again, ripping at its head, then at its back. Blood and entrails mixed with the mud that caked her muzzle. She clamped her jaws on the rabbit's shoulder and pulled—

"Storm! *Storm!*" Mickey slammed into her shoulder, making her stumble. In shock, Storm let the rabbit fall from her jaws.

"What's wrong with you?" Mickey was in her face now, barking furiously.

Storm's head spun. She blinked hard, staring down at the prey she'd caught.

There was almost nothing left of it to take back to the Pack. The rabbit between her forepaws was in shreds, its flesh torn and pulped into the ground. What remained of it wasn't even worth eating.

With a wrench of horror and shame in her belly, Storm raised her head. Mickey's shoulders were hunched with fury, and his lips were drawn back from his teeth. Storm shivered with appalled misery.

What have I done? How could I let Mickey down like this?

"Fierce Dogs," muttered Woody behind him. "What can you say? No surprise there."

At once rage fizzed through her bloodstream again, and Storm had to take a sharp breath and hold herself still to keep herself from turning on the other dog. Her whole body quivered with the effort. *Why can't I ever control myself? Maybe Woody's right!*

What had gotten her so worked up, after all? A dog being nice to her? A dog expressing some affection and concern? And that had thrown her into such a rage, she'd take it out on this helpless piece of prey . . . ?

Storm's heart was thundering in her ribs, and her head hurt as if her skull were about to split, but she licked her jaws and managed to control herself. *I won't snap at Woody; that would only prove him right.* Determinedly she turned away from him, crouched low in front of Mickey, and whined softly. After a moment, as he glared down at her, she rolled over to expose her belly.

"I'm sorry, Mickey." She found his eyes and blinked beseech-ingly. "I'm sorry, I was distracted. It won't happen again, I swear."

Mickey was breathing hard, but at last he relaxed and sat back on his haunches. He nodded. "All right, Storm. Just make sure it doesn't." His tail tapped, and he cast an anxious look at the remains of the rabbit, as if he couldn't help himself.

"It won't," she pleaded. "I promise."

"All right." He stood up and stepped back as Storm rolled back onto her paws and scrambled upright, her flanks still shud-dering. "The rabbit's not worth taking back, and there's a heavy scent of prey ahead. Let's find what's making it, and take a good meal home for the Pack, yes?"

Woody yipped his agreement, clearly relieved that the awful moment was over—*though no dog could be as relieved as I am*, thought Storm remorsefully. But as she turned with him to follow Mickey, she saw Whisper racing toward them. His eyes glittered with fear, and his whole body trembled.

Oh no, thought Storm with an inward groan. *Not again* . . .

Her worst fears were realized when he made straight for her, flinging himself close to her flank. As he slithered to a halt, he trembled against her.

Storm flinched away, angry. Why did he have to act like this, right now, and in front of Woody and Mickey? All the same, she couldn't help a pang of concern as she stared down at the gray dog. There was genuine terror in his eyes, and tremors ran through his muscles.

"What's happened?" she whined, trying to keep the irritation from her voice. *This day surely can't get any worse. . . .*

Whisper huddled even tighter against her, if that was possible. His voice shook as he whimpered.

"I followed the prey scent, Storm. I followed it all the way. And then I had to stop, I couldn't go farther because it was right in front of me!"

"What, Whisper, *what?*"

He gulped, and licked his chops. "A giantfur!"

CHAPTER EIGHTEEN

"What do we do, Mickey? Follow the prey, or retreat?" Woody tilted his head at the black-and-white Farm Dog.

Mickey licked his jaws. Woody was watching him carefully, and Whisper even more so. The gray dog was still shivering against Storm's flank, and she had to fight the desire to bat him away like an annoying pup.

At last Mickey gave a nod. "Let's go forward. Very carefully, though. We'll take it slowly and keep our noses sharp."

"But the giantfur . . ." moaned Whisper.

"They're not a threat to dogs. Not unless we disturb them, or attack them. If we give the giantfur a wide berth, and don't act threatening, we should be fine." Mickey turned and trotted in the direction the prey trail led them, and Woody fell in behind him.

Storm sighed and glanced down at Whisper. She could still feel the tremor of his muscles against her own flesh, and watching his wide, scared eyes, she felt her heart melt a little. *He only wants to help. I didn't have to be so harsh.*

"Come on," she said, giving him a nudge with her shoulder. "We're safest when we're all together, and I'll protect you if the giantfur attacks. Let's catch up with the others."

His gaze lowered in shame. "I'm not sure I can do this, Storm."

"Of course you can," she told him. "Remember, there's no Fear-Dog! There's not some Spirit Dog making you feel afraid; you can control your own fear."

Whisper brightened. "You're right." His tongue lolled as he glanced up at her. "You're right, Storm. And you always know exactly what to say."

If only you knew, she thought glumly. "Let's go, then."

As the dogs moved past the desolation of the skeleton forest and into greener land, Storm at last managed to shake off Whisper, and he fell back to walk with Woody. Storm bounded to catch up with Mickey, who gave her a sidelong glance. His nostrils were flared wide.

"The prey scent is stronger now, Storm." His eyes were bright with nervous anticipation. "Can you smell it?"

"Oh yes." Storm pricked her ears forward, frowning. "There's something else, though."

"And not just the giantfur," agreed Mickey. "Can you smell the blood? Whatever the prey is, it's hurt. And there's another animal I can't identify."

The softer, grassy ground was bliss on Storm's paw pads. She stepped carefully between tussocks, trying to avoid dry leaves and twigs. She couldn't make any sudden noises; they were so close to the giantfur now, they had to be even more careful.

Hesitantly, Mickey prowled around a thicket of flowering scrub. Storm saw his legs stiffen, and she hurried to his side.

He nodded at a hollow beneath the bush. "I knew I smelled something else."

Storm stared at the dead creature that lay there, half chewed. It was the strangest prey she'd ever laid eyes on. It was big—smaller but stockier than a deer—and its hide was covered in sparse prickly hair. The tail was barely worth the name. Its enormous head was turned slightly toward them, so that Storm could see two tiny half-open eyes and two curving fangs curling up from its lower jaw.

What was most noticeable, though, was how very delicious it smelled. Storm gave a shuddering sigh of longing, and drool gathered in her mouth.

"A tusknose!" exclaimed Woody from behind them. "I've seen those in the forest before, but not often."

"And it's fresh." Mickey licked his jaws as they gathered around to stare.

Woody cocked his head, and pawed carefully at the tusknose's stubby tail. "I'm not sure. I've got a feeling we should leave it alone."

Whisper nodded vigorously. "Yes. The giantfur scent is stronger than ever!"

"It's been here recently." Mickey took two paces back from the corpse of the tusknose. "This must be its prey."

"And if you ask me," added Whisper, "that smells like the same giantfur Storm saved me from last Ice Wind. When I was trapped by the tree outside its cave."

Storm nodded, reluctantly. "I think you're right, Whisper. The scent is the same."

Mickey shook out his fur. "Right. I think the only sensible course of action is to leave this. Big as it is, it's not worth getting in a fight with a giantfur."

He'd already turned to pad away, but Storm bounded after him. "Wait, Mickey!"

She strained back toward the tusknose, her nostrils widening

as she sniffed it. Its odor filled her skull, teasing her with its rich-
ness, and she realized drool was escaping from the corner of her
jaws. She licked her chops.

"It's prey," she said, turning to Mickey with a pleading expression. "And it's lying there as if the Forest-Dog gave it to us. We
didn't even have to chase it down!"

"No, Storm," said Mickey firmly. "That's not a good idea."

Storm looked from him to Woody. She vividly remembered
her moment of mad rage, when she'd deprived the Pack of a rabbit through her own temper. And here was something that would
more than make up for it. . . .

"We'd be crazy to leave this!" she blurted at last.

Mickey had opened his jaws to argue when Whisper stepped
forward. "Storm's right," he whined.

That wasn't surprising, she thought with an inward sigh. But
now Woody was changing his mind and growling in agreement,
too, the scent of the tusknose drawing him in.

"Come on, Mickey. It's free food for the Pack!"

"I still don't think—" began Mickey.

"But the rest of us agree it's a good idea." Woody cocked his
head. "And the giantfur isn't here to complain."

Mickey still looked hesitant, but at last he pawed the ground thoughtfully, and nodded. "Supposing you're right—who's going to drag this enormous creature back to camp?"

"I will," said Storm at once. "I can do it by myself!"

"Don't be a silly pup," snapped Mickey, a little irritably. "If we do this, Woody and Whisper and I will each take a turn. It's true it would make a good meal, though, and one the Pack desperately needs. Just promise me—if anything happens, we drop the tusk-nose and run."

"Absolutely," said Woody, and Whisper nodded energetically.

I'm taking this tusknose no matter what, Storm promised herself secretly.

"I'll go get the tusknose," she murmured. "You three wait here for now."

Carefully, one paw at a time, Storm crept back to the hollow. Despite her excitement, she couldn't repress the throb of fear in her veins. When she reached the dip and began to edge cautiously down the slope, the warning tingle in her fur almost brought her to a halt.

This is a serious thing you're doing, Storm. Don't mess it up. It could end in a lot worse than humiliation. . . .

The reek of the giantfur was overwhelming now, almost blotting out even the tantalizing scent of the tusknose. If she didn't know better, Storm would think the giantfur was right there with her, looming over her. . . .

The crash of undergrowth was so sudden, and so loud, every one of her muscles froze. Storm twisted on her haunches and cowered.

Oh, Sky-Dogs, it really is looming over me!

The giantfur's narrow snout was barely a squirrel-tail's length from her own—and small it might be, but it was open in a snarl that showed rows of ferocious teeth. Its black eyes glittered with surprise and fury. As Storm stared up, horrified and quite incapable of moving, the giantfur reared up on its hind legs and roared—and that was when Storm saw them, huddled at their mother's paws . . .

Two small giantfurs!

Storm's innards plummeted with a hideous shock of terror. *This was a mistake!*

A huge mistake, a *fatal* one. Every dog knew that mother giantfurs were at their most dangerous with their cubs around. *How could I not have foreseen this? Storm, you fool!*

Oh, Forest-Dog, save my stupid skin!

"Storm, *run!*"

From the lip of the hollow, Mickey's panicked bark finally

snapped her out of her funk. Scrambling to her paws, Storm turned tail and fled, just as the giantfur's long claws swiped the air where her head had been. She felt the *swoosh* of their passing like the touch of Ice Wind on her skin, and then she was running for her life.

She was petrified of tripping, sliding, falling. The whole earth shook with the thunder of the giantfur's paws as it lumbered after her. And as huge and ungainly as it looked, it was shockingly fast. Storm's panting breath rasped in her throat; she could barely fill her lungs for terror.

Ahead she could see the haunches of her hunting partners as they too fled. Whisper was trying to turn back, trying to bark encouragement to her, but Mickey nipped his rump to drive him on. *Good*, she managed to think. *I don't need Whisper being stupid on top of everything else!*

Mickey seemed to be heading for the vast swath of the dead forest, and Storm was for a moment afraid that he'd run there— *the giantfur will easily find us among those skeleton trees!*—but at the last moment he veered away and bolted toward a patch of birch and mountain ash. There was no time for the dogs to think as they plunged in among the slender trunks—they could only dodge and swerve and run, but the giantfur was not giving up. It pounded after them, bellowing its rage, and Storm realized quickly that this was no good. The trees were too sparse to provide any kind of cover.

She was running out of breath and strength; how must Whisper be coping? Just as she thought that, she heard Woody's frantic bark.

"Wrong way! We're leading it to the camp! Turn back!"

The dogs ducked, twisted, and ran again, the glossy black monster still lumbering swiftly after them. Storm realized with a bolt of horror: *It's going to catch us!*

Her vision was blurred with exhaustion, but she managed to make out a low line of dark green against the yellow grassland. With a last burst of energy, she gave a hoarse bark to alert the others, and sprinted ahead. They followed her as she hurtled toward a scrubby patch of bushes. As she drew closer she could see the dark green leaves, the dots of pink flowers.

"Get under there!" she howled, skidding to a stop.

Woody and Mickey didn't hesitate, diving in among the twisted, thorny branches. Whisper was struggling, running as fast as he could, but Storm could see the whites of his eyes as the giantfur rose behind him. As Whisper stumbled, Storm darted forward, seized the scruff of his neck and flung him under the bush. She saw a flash of long, lethal claws as she leaped herself, and then she was crawling into the shadows of branches, dragging herself by her foreclaws, panting harsh, agonized breaths.

Thorns dug into her hide, stabbed her skin, but she didn't care. Her flanks heaved as she lurched, struggling, farther into the scrub. Ahead in the gloom she could make out the others: Woody's patchy brown fur, Whisper's gray coat, and the stark black-and-white of Mickey. They were all cringing against the earth, staring back at her with wide white eyes.

"It knows we're in here!" Woody twisted his head to stare up as the sounds of crashing echoed through the branches.

"It won't follow," gasped Storm, "I hope."

"Hope the thorns keep it out." Mickey's muzzle was bleeding from a deep scratch, but he didn't seem to notice or care.

A branch cracked violently, and showers of leaves pattered around the dogs. They all flinched.

"It's coming in," whimpered Whisper. "It's coming!"

Storm cringed lower as the pounding thud of the giantfur's paws vibrated right through her belly. Another roar made her shut her eyes tight. More branches splintered and creaked, and she heard a deep guttural snuffling sound.

"It knows!" whined Woody again.

"Yes, it does, but it'll give up soon." Storm hoped against hope that she was right.

And then, quite suddenly, the crashing faltered. With a grunt and a last bellow of anger, the giantfur stopped tearing at the bushes. Storm heard it thud down onto all four paws, and then the fading echo as it turned and pounded away, back toward its cubs.

"Oh, thank the Forest-Dog," gasped Mickey as silence fell.

"That," said Woody, heaving a sigh, "was closer than I ever wanted to be to a giantfur."

Storm let her head flop to the dusty ground, and closed her eyes, panting to get her breath back. "I'm so sorry. Bad move."

"Oh Storm, never mind that!" The eager bark was all too recognizable. "You saved my life *again*!"

She blinked her eyes open, and stared dully. Whisper was gazing right into her face, his expression worshipful.

"Storm, you are just the *best*!"

She gave a quiet groan, and shut her eyes tight once more.

Oh, Sky-Dogs. Is it too late to throw him to the giantfur?

CHAPTER NINETEEN

Storm's leg muscles ached and her paw pads stung as she trudged back into the camp behind Mickey and Woody, with Whisper trailing at her heels. It wasn't just the scrapes and bruises from escaping the giantfur that made her whole body hurt, she thought: It had been the sheer gut-churning terror. She felt as if she might never dare to leave her den again.

That will pass, she thought. *But I do feel like the most foolish dog ever born.*

"In the name of the Earth-Dog, what happened?" Lucky trotted to meet them, his whiskers quivering with concern. "You all look as if you've been running from Lightning!"

"That's how we feel," groaned Woody.

"Was it the foxes?" Lucky's eyes were bright with alarm. "Or did you run into more—" He shut his jaws as his gaze slanted toward Storm, and he swallowed his next words.

Storm's head drooped with exhaustion and misery. She knew exactly what he'd been about to say: *Did you run into more Fierce Dogs?*

Mickey padded forward, his shoulders hunched and his head low with shame. "I'm sorry, Lucky. The truth is, we tried to take prey from a giantfur. Needless to say, we didn't succeed."

Lucky could only stare at him for long moments, as if lost for words. At last he exploded: "Whose ridiculous idea was *that?*"

"Every dog's." Mickey sighed with resignation. "We all agreed to give it a try. It was an honest mistake, Lucky, and we won't make it again."

"It wasn't every dog," growled Woody. "Storm talked us into it. It was her idea."

Lucky turned to him, his muzzle curling. "Don't lie to me, Woody. Storm wouldn't suggest anything so stupid. Are you blaming her because she's a Fierce Dog? Because I'm sick of—"

"No." Storm shoved past Woody and stood foursquare in front of Lucky. But she couldn't meet his eyes; she could only stare dismally at the ground, her tail trembling against her rump. *Who knew blades of grass could be so fascinating? Right now I want to look at them forever. . . .*

"Storm?" Lucky cocked his ears expectantly.

"I—" She coughed to clear her throat. "It's true, Beta. It was my idea. And I kept pressing Mickey to do it."

"No! It wasn't Storm!" The high bark came from behind her.

I don't believe this. She turned, startled. *Not again!*

But there he was at her shoulder, the adoring gray dog who was fast becoming her worst nightmare. "It was *my* idea," announced Whisper. "It was all my fault, Beta."

Storm wanted to bite Whisper's ears off. She snarled at him. "Stop lying for me! I don't want you to! What is it with you, Whisper?"

"That's enough." Lucky's cold voice made them all turn quickly back to him. His normally gentle eyes were contemptuous. "All four of you should have known better. I'm disappointed in you." His stare seemed to focus particularly on her, thought Storm with a sinking heart. *But that's fair enough.*

"You'll all have to hunt again this evening," Lucky went on. "I don't care how tired you are; the Pack can't go hungry just because you acted rashly. *Incompetently.* Go and get some rest; you're going to need it." With a dismissive flick of his tail, he stalked away, stiff with anger.

Woody, Whisper, and Mickey slunk off, heads low and tails

clamped to their rumps, but Storm lingered, staring after Lucky.

I've let him down so badly.

Making a sudden decision, she sprang to catch up with him. "Lucky! Beta, I mean."

He glanced over his shoulder. To her relief, his face was no longer filled with fury, but if anything, the disappointment in his eyes hurt her more. Trying to ignore the gnawing sensation of shame in her gut, Storm padded to his side.

Humbly, she lowered her forequarters. "Beta. May I speak with you?"

He looked at her askance. "All right," he told her gruffly. "Don't imagine I've forgotten the giantfur, though. How could you be so rash, Storm?"

"I know. And I'm sorry." She thumped her tail miserably against the earth.

"Follow me." Without another word he set off in the direction of the pond, and she hurried to obey him.

The water looked cool, dark, and delicious, fringed thickly with reeds, and Storm would have loved to plunge straight into it to soothe her paws, but she didn't dare. Instead she sat down obediently, head lowered, as Lucky walked forward to the edge of the pond to greet Twitch.

The three-legged dog lurched to his paws, returning Lucky's friendly licks. "You two look as if you want some privacy," he growled amicably. "I'll leave you to it."

"No, Twitch, stay." Lucky sat back on his haunches. "I think Third Dog should be part of this conversation. Don't you agree, Storm?"

I thought I could speak to you alone. . . . Her heart sank heavily, but she nodded. "Yes, Beta."

Lucky tilted his head to study her as Twitch lay down again, his eyes alert. "Storm," said Lucky, "if you're worried about something, you can tell me and Twitch. You know that, don't you?"

She hesitated, glancing from one to the other.

"Especially if you don't want to speak to Alpha directly," Lucky went on. "We can talk to her on your behalf, if it's something she needs to deal with. Yes?"

"Yes," muttered Storm. She dug her claws into the soft mud, scratching a deep groove.

"We'll always help you if we can," murmured Twitch. "That's what we're here for."

"It's really hard to explain." Storm raised her eyes to theirs at last, tormented. Her stomach felt like a giant knot inside her.

"Then take your time," offered Twitch.

Storm took a deep breath. Did she really want to speak out about this, after so much time spent chewing obsessively on it by herself?

"I've been having bad dreams," she blurted, before she could think any harder.

Lucky's ears pricked up, and he tilted his head.

"Go on," said Twitch.

Storm coughed to clear her throat. It was so hard to talk about it. "I dream about darkness. It's always no-sun, and there are . . . Fierce Dogs. And the Fear-Dog. I've . . . when I have these dreams, I wake up outside."

"What?" Twitch's eyes widened. "Outside your den?"

"Way outside it," she muttered. "I wake up right outside the camp. Quite a long way out, sometimes. I don't ever remember getting there."

Beta and Third Dog stared at her, waiting in silence for her to continue. Storm swallowed.

"I've been walking in my sleep," she confessed at last. "I don't understand how it happens, but it does." Her voice rose to a miserable whine. "And I don't know what it means."

Lucky frowned thoughtfully. "Has any other dog seen you do this?"

"Two dogs know." Storm's head sagged. "Please don't tell the others. Please."

Lucky shook his head. "Of course not, Storm," he said kindly. "Your secret's safe with us. Right, Twitch?"

"Absolutely," confirmed Third Dog. "This is nothing to worry about, Storm. Have you been gnawing at this? All dogs get bad dreams sometimes, and it's not the first time I've heard of dogs walking in their sleep." He paused, seemed to think hard for a moment, then murmured: "Tell us, Storm. Did you have one of these dreams the night the fox-pup was murdered?"

Storm took a pace back, feeling her neck fur bristle. *What's he implying?* she thought in a panic. But before she could think of a reply, Lucky padded forward.

"Don't look like that, Storm. Twitch didn't mean anything by that, did you?"

"Of course not," said Twitch hastily.

Storm let her back muscles relax slightly, but she furrowed her brow as she watched Lucky. Her Beta's eyes seemed distant, as if his mind was trying to unravel some intricate, impossible tangle of thoughts.

"What is it, Lucky?" she asked nervously. "What are you thinking?"

"Nothing." He looked away sharply, as if the still surface of the pond and its skittering water beetles were suddenly fascinating. "Look, Storm, neither of us thinks for a moment that you had anything to do with the fox-pup."

"Absolutely," agreed Twitch vigorously. "You're the last dog we'd suspect, Storm, and that's the truth."

"And your secret's safe with us." Lucky nuzzled her shoulder, then licked her ear comfortingly. "I'm glad you finally trusted us enough to tell us about your dreams."

"I'm sorry I didn't tell you before." Storm realized it was true. Already her burden seemed lighter, now that she'd shared it with Lucky and Twitch. *If things get worse, they'll know what to do. And I don't have to feel I'm keeping some terrible secret.*

"I understand why you didn't. And I understand why you're anxious, Storm, and I take it seriously, but please try not to worry." Lucky pressed his muzzle to her cheekbone. "Now, you'd better get some rest. I'm not letting you off of that extra hunt!"

As Storm trotted back to camp, there was a distinct spring in her step, and her heart felt lighter than it had in many journeys of the Sun-Dog.

They believed me, she thought. *They believed me, and they don't think I'm crazy or bad.*

Tonight I won't let Lucky down.

Evening birdsong filled the clearing as Lucky led the extra hunting party out of the camp, and late slanting sunlight filtered through the branches. Despite her exhaustion, Storm made sure she kept at her Beta's shoulder, her nostrils wide and all her senses alert.

It was typical of Lucky, she thought, that despite the late hunt being a punishment, he'd chosen to lead them himself. And in fact, he'd made the last-minute decision to leave Mickey and Woody behind.

"I know the four of you were trying to help the Pack when you raided that giantfur's prey," he'd told them, "but it was such a wrongheaded decision, I can't risk taking all of you out this time. I need to be sure I can trust you to work together properly. Without showing off," he'd added, with a pointed glance at Storm. "Best to separate you for now."

The four of them had looked appropriately cowed and sheepish, even though Lucky's fury had abated. *We really have learned our lesson*, thought Storm. *Now we just have to prove it to our Beta.*

Lucky had, however, insisted that Whisper come along. The

scout dog was fast, and surprisingly, he wasn't as tired as the others. Whisper, too, of course, had had a scolding from his Beta.

"It's loyal of you to stand up for Storm," Lucky had told him sternly, "but your loyalty was misplaced. Every dog must learn to stand on his own paws—and that includes you, Whisper. This hunt will be your chance to prove yourself."

And Whisper was very eager to do just that. "I'll show you what I'm worth, Beta, I promise. I won't let the Pack down!"

Though his eyes had been fixed on Lucky, Storm knew Whisper's words had been mostly for her ears. Now the gray dog was trotting ahead of them up the shoreline as they followed the coast of the Endless Lake. The Sun-Dog's evening light turned the water blood red and the sand to gold, and Storm loved the salty fragrance of the water in her nostrils. Behind her Bella and Snap paced energetically; Storm knew that they too found the Lake's air refreshingly sharp. It was lighter, somehow, than the air of the deep green woods, yet not nearly as bitter as the winds of the cliff top.

Maybe we'll catch some of those fat white birds unawares, she thought hopefully: *those ones that nest on the cliffs. Or if we go higher, maybe there will be rabbits.*

And this time I won't tear them to a pulp. Storm swallowed guiltily, but it was too beautiful an evening to brood about it, and her mood was not crushed for long.

"Here!" Whisper had stopped right below the rockface, and now he was standing foursquare, his head thrust forward as he scented the breeze. "Weasels, I think."

The other four dogs ran to catch up, and Lucky nodded approvingly. "There are definitely some around here. Nesting, maybe."

"So what are we waiting for?" said Snap, pricking her ears high. "Let's get digging!"

At the base of the cliff, where the dry sand was piled, the rocks and stones were loose, and with the claws of all five dogs working to rake them away, it was short work to expose the small tunnel. The smell of weasel grew stronger as they dug, and Whisper gave a yelp of satisfaction as they finally exposed the squirming creatures.

The weasels were agile and fast, the young ones almost fully grown, but after much darting and snapping—and dodging the weasels' tiny fangs—the dogs had managed to kill five of them. Lucky stood back in satisfaction, gazing at the tangle of small red corpses.

"It's enough." He nodded. "Together with what the other

hunting party brought back, this will feed the Pack for tonight."

"We should find more!" Despite the lateness, Storm felt fired up for more hunting, her blood buzzing with the excitement of the kill.

"No." Lucky nodded toward the Sun-Dog, who was curling up in a glow of radiance close to the horizon. "He'll be going to his rest soon, and we should get the prey back to camp before no-sun."

"It's strange that Sun-Dog wants to sleep in the Endless Lake," murmured Snap, gazing wistfully at the Spirit Dog's gorgeous colors. His tail lay in a golden path across the waves.

Bella gave a small huff of laughter. "There's no accounting for the whims of the Spirit Dogs," she said brusquely. "Beta's right, we should get the prey home."

The hunters turned back to pick up the weasels, but as Lucky ducked to lift one, he hesitated. Then, abruptly, he snapped his head up.

"What's that?" His nostrils snuffed the air, and his ears were pricked high as they could go, straining to hear something.

"The scent of the lake," offered Storm, sniffing it appreciatively. "You know that."

"No, Storm. There's something else."

All of the dogs stood very still, casting around for a hint of what Lucky had detected. Storm gasped as she caught the scent. *Yes.* Beneath the salty tang of the Lake, there was a sweet, spicy fragrance. A deer-scent, but with something more.

"You're right," she exclaimed, stretching her muzzle to find a further trace of that elusive, tempting scent.

"Look! There!" Lucky sprang a pace toward the cliff, and stared upward.

The others followed his gaze, and Storm took a shocked breath. As the Sun-Dog settled even lower, his light was shining on the rockface, turning it to an almost liquid gold. And there, at the very crest of the cliff, stood a deer.

Its head was raised, and it seemed to be looking straight at the dogs, but it was unafraid. For long heartbeats it stood unmoving, silhouetted in the amber glow; then quite casually, it turned and cantered elegantly away from the cliff top.

"The Golden Deer," barked Lucky hoarsely. "This time I'm sure of it!"

"But Beta," objected Bella. "It's almost no-sun time!"

"We have to go after it," he insisted, staring longingly at the top of the rockface. "What if it's the real Golden Deer and I don't take the chance? What would the Wind-Dogs think of me?"

"Or of any of us," agreed Snap, ignoring Bella's skeptical stare.

"I'm with you, Beta. No-sun or not, we have to follow it."

For once, Storm's sympathies lay with Bella, despite the tempting beauty of the deer. "We can't abandon this prey," she said, nudging the weasels with her nose, "just to go chasing after a shadow."

"No, of course not." Lucky's eyes were alight with energy and enthusiasm; he looked as if he could take a flying leap straight to the top of the cliff. For an instant, Storm was afraid he'd actually try it. "Storm, you and Bella and Whisper should take the prey back to camp. Snap and I will go after the deer. Tell Alpha and Twitch not to hold back prey-sharing for us." He exchanged a hopeful glance with Snap. "We're going to follow the trail of the Golden Deer—till we lose it forever, or catch it for the Pack!"

Storm found herself lost for words. She could understand Lucky's overwhelming urge to pursue the deer. She'd have liked to do it herself—but she had sworn that on this hunt, there would be no wild plans, no letting the Pack down for the sake of excitement. So even if that meant missing an adventure led by Lucky himself, she would obey him.

At last, with reluctance, Storm dipped her head. "All right, Beta. We'll tell Alpha what's happened."

"You're crazy, both of you," Bella told Lucky and Snap crisply.

"But good luck—I hope you catch your ghost deer soon!"

Lucky and Snap dipped their heads in acknowledgment, then bounded toward the far end of the bay where the cliff sloped closest to the sand. A little heavy of heart, Storm turned away to help Bella and Whisper pick up the weasels.

The three of them had just set off back the way they'd come, in the direction of the camp, when Storm heard Lucky's wild baying howl.

"Speed up, Snap! Let's run. The Golden Deer has bolted!"

CHAPTER TWENTY

Stars were starting to wink and sparkle in a dark blue sky above the treetops as Storm and Bella approached the camp, Whisper trailing behind them. However hard Storm might listen in the clear cool air, there was no sound of other pawsteps behind them, no crunch of twigs.

"Don't worry, Storm." Bella nudged her. "Beta and Snap will be fine. They're a stubborn pair. They'll probably still be chasing after that so-called Golden Deer until it's long gone, and they're both exhausted."

"I know," said Storm through her jawful of weasel. "But this is going to be a hard one to explain to Alpha...."

Just as they padded over the border, Alpha appeared from her den and walked toward them, her sleek pale coat gleaming in the starlight. Her silhouette was very distended now. *It can't be long till the pups come, surely*, thought Storm.

"Where's Beta?" Alpha lifted her ears and looked from Bella to Storm, to Whisper behind them. "What's happened?" Her voice was stern, but there was genuine concern in her eyes.

Storm laid down her prey. "He spotted the Golden Deer, Alpha."

"Or he thought he did." Bella hunched her shoulders as she dropped her own weasels. "Anyway, he and Snap didn't want to miss the chance. He said they'll chase it till they lose the scent, or catch the deer."

Alpha's eyes brightened in her slender face. "Oh! That . . . that makes me very happy. Beta's taking the Wind-Dogs and their favor seriously, if he hopes to catch the Golden Deer." She sighed, and gave Bella a rather pointed glance. "I'm not sure every other dog does."

"He'll do his best to find it, Alpha, I know that." Storm was determined to steer the talk away from Bella's skepticism. "But he asked that we go ahead with prey-sharing. He and Snap don't know when they'll return."

"Then we'll do that." Sweet held her head high with pleasure as she turned to summon the Pack. "All dogs, to me! It's time to share the good fortune the Forest-Dog and the Wind-Dogs have provided."

As the Pack gathered, Storm licked and nibbled at her paws, loosening the sand that had stuck between the pads. One by one, as always, the dogs stepped up under Alpha's benevolent gaze to choose their prey; it wasn't the biggest feast they'd ever been able to share, but thanks to the extra hunting patrol there was enough to fill their bellies. At least, Storm mused, there were no arguments tonight about the rankings, or the order in which dogs ate—but something nagged at her, something that felt quite wrong. At last she realized: Of course it felt odd to share prey without Lucky's presence.

When it was over, and all the dogs had eaten their fill, she laid her head on her paws and sighed, glancing up at the stars. *Sky-Dogs, look after Lucky and Snap. Don't let them go running off the edge of any cliffs. Because I wouldn't be surprised if they keep too much of an eye on the Golden Deer, and not nearly enough on where they're going. . . .*

The Pack was settling in to sleep, one after another, padding off to their dens or simply curling up on patches of softer ground in the balmy New-Leaf night. Twisting her head, Storm caught sight of Whisper. He lay not half a rabbit-chase away, his eyes riveted on her.

Oh no. Her gut sank. *How long is this going to go on?*

With a sigh, Storm got to her paws. She didn't want to sleep out here, but nor did she want to go to her den. Whisper would be bound to track her either way—and if she was going to walk in her sleep again, she didn't want the annoying dog to be a witness to her weakness.

I'll do exactly what I've been telling dogs I do, all along. I'll go for a walk.

It didn't seem like a bad option at all. The dark sky was beautiful, the breeze gentle, and the scents of the forest were all around her; there was no sense of danger in the night. And, Storm realized, if she walked long enough to tire herself out, when she got back she might actually stay put in her sleep for once.

Hesitating just outside camp, Storm looked toward the forest, and then up to the cliff top. Moon was still on High Watch there, serving out her punishment for something she hadn't done. Irritation nibbled at Storm's gut again, but she didn't want to spoil such a lovely night with thoughts of betrayal within the Pack. The least she could do, anyway, was climb up to the ridge and visit with Moon. The Farm Dog would probably appreciate the company.

Storm could feel the wind strengthening even through the dense tree thickets as she bounded up the steep slope. There was definitely more of an edge to the breeze up here, despite it being

New Leaf, and once again she felt sorry for Moon, banished to this lonely spot. As the ground leveled out Storm picked up her pace, and she broke into a loose-limbed run as she reached the top of the cliff. *It's good to stretch my legs properly, now that we have that overcautious new hunting strategy. . . .*

She skidded to a surprised halt as she caught sight of Moon's pale shape. There was another dog with her, and both were sitting gazing out over the gleaming blackness of the Endless Lake. Storm trotted up to them, seeing with surprise that Breeze was the second dog. Storm's ears pricked up at the sight: surely it was a good sign that a dog from Twitch's Pack was so friendly with Moon.

"Hello, Moon. Hello, Breeze! Can't you sleep either?"

"Not really," barked Breeze softly as Moon licked Storm in greeting. "I'm worried about Snap and Beta. Dogs shouldn't wander off on night hunts, you know. Especially with only two of them. It's a bit rash, don't you think?"

"Now, Breeze." Moon nuzzled her companion's shoulder, then turned to Storm. "I've already told her, Storm, there's nothing to worry about. Beta and Snap will be just fine. They have each other, and they're both smart dogs. They're a little overexcited about the Golden Deer, that's all."

"I'm sure you're right." Breeze sighed, then turned to look down at the shoreline once more. Far below them the Endless Lake was calm, its white-edged waves small and gentle as they rushed and whispered ceaselessly against the sand. "I suppose I should go to my den and get some sleep."

"That's a good idea," Moon told her. "By the time you wake at sunup, I'm sure Snap will be curled up beside you. Don't worry."

"All right." Breeze yawned luxuriously, stretched her forelegs, then padded back toward the slope that led to the camp. "Don't you take too long either, Storm," she called over her shoulder. "There'll be more hard hunting tomorrow, and you must be tired."

Storm and Moon watched the brown dog make her way down the rough path till she was out of sight. Moon sighed. "Don't let Breeze's worries get to you, Storm. Snap and Lucky will both be fine."

"I know." Storm gave her an affectionate lick.

It surprised her, Storm realized, how fond she'd grown of Moon. At first the Farm Dog hadn't liked Storm at all, and had made her feel unwelcome in the Pack, especially when Storm and her brothers clashed with Moon's own pups; but that was when Lucky and Mickey had first brought home the three Fierce Dog pups. They'd been the first Fierce Dogs the Pack had ever met without being attacked, and it hadn't been easy for any dog to adjust to their presence. Even later, when Storm was growing up awkward and unaware of her own strength, Moon had often been riled.

Storm had been wary of Moon, too, but now she couldn't think why she ever had been. Moon could be snappy and ferocious, but that was usually in defense of Thorn and Beetle. And ever since Storm had helped save Moon's mate Fiery from the bad longpaws—even though Fiery hadn't made it in the end—Moon had been far warmer toward her. Acceptance, and maybe even friendship, from the sharp-tongued dog meant more to Storm than she could put into words.

"By the way, Storm," growled Moon into the companionable silence, "I want you to know something. I don't think for an instant that you had anything to do with that fox-pup."

Storm felt a rush of warm gratitude. "Thanks for saying so, Moon. For what it's worth, I know you didn't either."

"No," said Moon slowly. "I couldn't have done such a thing. I hate foxes, you know that. But to kill a little one, in cold blood? I'd be doing what they did to me, and how would that make me any better than them?"

"I know," said Storm, butting Moon's neck gently.

Moon gave another sigh and lay down with her head on her paws. "I hope Alpha and Beta's pups will be safe and happy. I'd hate it if anything were to happen to them. It's something no Mother- or Father-Dog should ever have to go through."

"I'm sure Beta and Alpha will take care of them," Storm reassured her. "Protect them with their lives, in fact." She huffed a laugh. "Beta's already so overprotective, and they haven't even been born yet!"

Moon chuckled. "Fiery was just the same. I was hardly allowed to set paw outside the den, in case I tripped over a twig." Her expression grew wistful. "I'm so happy for Alpha and Beta, but I can't help feeling sad when I remember Fuzz and Fiery. Fuzz was so very tiny when he was killed."

"And you still miss Fiery, of course." Storm stared out at the Endless Lake, feeling a little awkward. She'd been fond of Fiery, and she'd admired him, but Moon's obvious emotion was unsettling. Perhaps she could steer the conversation onto happier times for the pair. . . . "How did you two meet?"

"Oh! You won't be surprised to hear that he came to my rescue." Moon laughed softly.

"Some dog attacked you?"

"Something did, but not a dog. It wasn't an enemy any of us

could fight. My Pack was attacked by a sickness. Who knows how these things begin?" Moon shook her head. "Some dogs died—the older ones, and the youngest. Even some of the strongest." Moon's voice caught, and she swallowed. "My sister, Star, died. And my parent-dogs—our Pack's Alpha and Beta."

"Oh, Moon." Storm's heart turned over in her chest. She knew how it felt to lose family. . . . "How terrible."

"It was." Shaking her head, Moon licked her jaws. "I grew sick eventually myself. But Fiery and his Pack, the beginnings of this Pack, were living in the next territory, with the half wolf as their leader. Fiery defied his own Alpha, the half wolf, to help us. He brought plants that helped bring down fever, and he tended to dogs who were too sick even to drink water. He protected us when we were too weak to defend our own territory. He was kind. And brave."

Storm pricked her ear curiously. "And Fiery never got sick? The thing didn't attack him?"

"No. Fiery thought that perhaps he was impervious to it. He remembered that when he was a very small pup, the Pack he was in was attacked by a similar enemy, the same kind of sickness. And he survived when many dogs didn't. So he thought that perhaps that enemy could never hurt him."

"He was always a strong dog." Storm gave Moon's jaw a comforting nuzzle.

"Yes. But you know, he told me later that he used to worry about it. About surviving when so many of his Pack died. When he was young, he was afraid he'd somehow betrayed his Pack, and that the invisible thing had left him alone because of that."

"That couldn't be true!" Storm blinked in surprise.

"No, of course not. Fiery understood that, once he was a grown dog, but pups worry about things like that, don't they?" Moon gave her a glance that was slightly knowing. "Some pups worry that there's something bad inside them, something they can't help."

Storm licked her jaws. *That sounds all too familiar. . . .*

"Anyway," Moon went on, "by the time the sickness passed, I barely had a Pack to lead. I'd become Alpha when my Father-Dog died, but I'd lost all my love for leadership by then. Fiery pleaded with the half wolf to let those of us who were left join his Pack. Without Fiery, the half wolf would never have taken us in. He'd already kept his distance till the invisible enemy had gone. The half wolf didn't want sickness in his own Pack, and that was understandable."

"And it sounds very like him," muttered Storm, remembering

their ruthless former Alpha.

"Yes, but it did make sense. He made the right decision for his own Pack, but Fiery had sympathy for mine. He saved many dogs, Storm, including me. Fiery hunted prey for us when no other dog could do it. He found water for us. He even did Omega jobs, like clearing out bedding that smelled bad. If it hadn't been for Fiery, I think we would *all* have died." Moon sighed sadly. "That's when I fell in love with him. He was so very brave, and he cared so much."

"Brave dogs are good dogs," said Storm, to buy time as her mind picked over the implications of the story. "And caring dogs too." *But why in the name of the Earth-Dog do brave and caring dogs have to take mates? Can't they just look after every dog in a Pack? A permanent mate takes up so much of a dog's time and attention!* She shook her head, mystified. *And as for pups . . .*

She couldn't bite back the question. "Moon, why do dogs take mates at all?"

Moon gave her a surprised glance. "Don't you know?"

"Well, I know a *bit*," muttered Storm. "I mean, Packs need pups, don't they? And I suppose some dogs in a Pack must be good at all that fuss and bother of raising them. But spending all your time with just one dog—doesn't it get boring?"

She nibbled the side of her mouth, afraid that she'd offended Moon, but the Farm Dog's reaction wasn't at all what she'd expected. Moon gave a sudden, barking laugh.

"Oh, Storm! You're so young, but you'll find out." Moon gave her a fond sweep of her tongue. "It's true that some dogs don't take mates. And the ones that do, don't always stick to one mate their whole lives. And there are even dogs who don't want pups, or can't have them. But sometimes there's only one possible mate for a dog. You know as soon as your gazes meet, or as soon as you catch his scent, that he's the dog you are meant to be with. It might take a lifetime, but you'll know. And no other dog will do for you after that." Her eyes grew distant and sad again. "I know I'll never have another mate now that Fiery's gone."

"I don't see why not," said Storm awkwardly. "You might. You don't know that. Some dog might appear and . . ." She shook herself vigorously. "Anyway, that's not how I'm going to live my life. It's not the way for me, I'm afraid. I mean, I'm not *afraid*. It's what I *want*. To be my own dog."

Moon gave her a thoughtful look, one that held a trace of amusement, and Storm fidgeted and averted her eyes.

"Don't plan out your life too carefully, Storm," said Moon

gently. "You never know what might come along to change your path."

"I think a dog should know what she wants, though," said Storm. "And I'm very sure of my path. But thank you, Moon." She nuzzled the Farm Dog's ear, suddenly embarrassed. "I didn't . . . I mean, I hope I didn't hurt your feelings. Saying what I did about mates?"

"Of course not." Moon wore that amused expression again, the one that unsettled Storm. "Why don't you go back to camp now, and get some sleep? You must be tired. And Breeze was right, you'll be out hunting again tomorrow."

Yes, thought Storm, *and I think I'm actually tired enough now to sleep properly.* "I'll do that, I think. Good night, Moon."

As she turned away, her eye was caught by a movement, a flash of light far out on the Endless Lake. She hesitated, staring, and Moon rose to stand beside her and follow her gaze.

"That's not the Light House." Storm furrowed the skin above her eyes, and twitched her whiskers. "It can't move. Can it?"

There were lights on a dark shape, and they seemed to be moving across the surface of the water. One red light blinked at the tail of the creature, one hovered above it like an eye, and there were irregular yellow lights on its flanks.

Storm had never seen anything like it. "Can that thing really be moving on the Endless Lake? Why doesn't it sink under the water?"

Moon shook her head slowly. "I don't know," she murmured, "but I think it might be a floatcage. A longpaw's creature, like a loudcage, but one that travels on the water."

"Like a loudbird travels through the air?" mused Storm. "I suppose it makes a kind of sense."

"I've seen small floatcages before, on the river," Moon told her. "Much smaller, with longpaw pups riding on them. But look at that one! If it's a floatcage, it's a very big one. See how far out on the lake it is?"

Together they watched in awe as the floatcage drifted on, following the line of the coast. It moved slowly, but always in the same direction, never coming closer to the shore.

"I don't like its eyes," said Storm after a while, shivering at the constant glow of the lights on its body. "It looks as if it's watching us."

"It's moving away, though," Moon observed. "It'll be out of sight soon. And I must say, I'll be glad."

Storm gave a huge shudder, trying to release the tension in her hide. At once she was overwhelmed by a yawn. "I really do need to go back to my den," she said apologetically. "Will you be all right out here?"

"Don't worry about me. I'm getting used to it. It's quite peaceful up here, in a way." Moon stretched, and sat up. "And I'm wide awake now. I'll watch for more floatcages. If those creatures are going to be a threat to my pups and the Pack, I don't want to let them out of my sight."

Snarling, Storm snapped her jaws at her enemies, but her fangs closed on thin air. It was like biting shadow, or dark water. Nothing was there for her to seize. She couldn't wound a shadow, or take hold of its scruff and fling it to the ground. Yet as she twisted, growling, to face another attacker, she felt vicious shadow-teeth bite into her flank, like shards of ice.

It wasn't a fair fight. She couldn't harm the shadow-dogs, but they could hurt her!

She spun to try to drive the dog away, but instantly another one lunged, throwing itself bodily onto her back. Storm writhed, snapping, but there was no shifting it—the shadow clung to her with claws that dug down to her bones. Its weight was forcing her to the ground—how could a ghost weigh so heavily on her? It was impossible to move. Down, down she sank, the shadow spreading over her, its teeth in her neck and its claws in her sides. *The shadow was sinking* through her! *Darkness, seeping down through fur and skin and muscle until it reached her bones. The sensation was unbearable, something between an itch, a tickle, and sheer pain; yet she had to bear it, because she could do nothing to stop it. What was the point of this? What were they doing to her?*

And she realized, with a bolt like icy fire to her brain:

They're driving the cold to my heart!

She could feel the dark frost inside her chest, oozing closer to her innermost core. Her heart thumped wildly at her rib cage, but it couldn't escape, and neither could she. The shadows were forcing it down with monstrous paws, filling her with the darkness—

Terrified, she rolled over, kicking frantically. She had to throw off this shadow! Impossible as it seemed, she had to dislodge it from her, get rid of it, kill it, no matter what. Because if she didn't—

Storm blinked open her eyes. Her heart was still thrashing wildly, her hackles erect, but she was on her paws, shaking uncontrollably, her tongue hanging out as she gasped and panted for breath.

Of course. I'm outside camp. Again.

And farther than ever from her den, she realized with a wrench of horror. Her muscles ached and she could swear she felt the scratches and bites and wounds on her hide. *It's as if I really have been fighting another dog,* she thought.

The images and sensations were fading fast, though, and she shook her fur to get rid of them faster. *Maybe I shouldn't do that, though. Maybe I should try to remember.*

Who had she been fighting? She couldn't picture that shadowy dog at all, though she felt the physical memory of its assault. All Storm could remember was that dark outline, the ghostly strength and agility of it.

"Storm, is that you?" Lucky's anxious bark shook her out of her awful reverie. "Are you all right?"

"Lucky!" Storm gasped, and swung around to peer into the forest. She could make out the shapes of Beta and Snap pacing toward her, on their way back to the camp. Trying not to let her legs shake, she walked forward to meet them.

"Storm, is everything all right at the camp?" Lucky stared at her very intently.

"Yes. Yes, it's fine." Storm lashed her tail, and peered again at the two dogs. They were empty-pawed, that was immediately obvious. "You didn't catch the Golden Deer, then? Did you lose the scent after all?"

"On the contrary, we followed the scent all the way back here." Lucky had to be exhausted, but there was still a gleam of wild excitement in his eyes. "The Wind-Dogs have led us in a dance, Storm—in a wide circle all around the camp." He eyed her more closely, and there was concern in his voice as he said, meaningfully, "Couldn't you sleep, Storm?"

She knew what he was trying to ask her: *Did you walk in your sleep again?* She glanced nervously at Snap, but the chase-dog didn't seem to have noticed anything odd in Lucky's line of questioning. Snap was watching them both with only casual interest.

"I . . . no, I couldn't sleep, not really," Storm blustered. "I think I was too excited, thinking about you two chasing the Golden Deer."

"I see." Lucky nodded, but there was a lingering worry in his expression.

Storm sat down, to rest her paws and also to conceal the trembling of her limbs. "You say the trail led back here?" she asked curiously.

"Yes. Strange, isn't it?" Snap lifted her nose, as if eager to find the scent again.

"So . . . you're still hunting it?" Storm got back to her paws, suddenly excited by the possible distraction.

"Oh yes," said Lucky, his tongue lolling happily. "We're not giving up on the Golden Deer now, not when we've come so close."

"I'll come with you," she told them. Her tail was wagging all by itself now, and her nerves buzzed with the thrill of the chase. Her aches and exhaustion fell away like water on a river-rabbit's fur. "I can smell it too!"

Lucky gave a low bark of agreement. "Good, Storm! If you can't sleep"— he gave her another pointed look—"there's nothing better than a nighttime hunt to take your mind off it."

Storm turned and followed Lucky as he bounded forward through the trees. Her head was suddenly clear, and her muscles felt as fresh as if she'd slept the night away.

We're going to hunt the Golden Deer!

CHAPTER TWENTY-ONE

Storm's long legs ate up the ground, her paws pounding fast and steadily. It felt so good to be racing at Lucky's side, to be joining him in this mad, wonderful hunt, Snap just a few paces behind them. Beneath her paw pads, forest litter and dry leaves became soft yielding meadow grass, and then sand, and then shelves of hard rock, but still the dogs ran. The scent of the Golden Deer was stronger than ever in her nostrils, making her light-headed with hope and excitement.

Once or twice the dogs' pawsteps faltered, as the trail seemed to dissipate and drift into nothing. But at a bark from Lucky they would sprint on.

"Don't you see it? The Golden Deer. There!"

They had been running for so long without finding anything that Storm was sure Lucky was imagining the creature; perhaps it was wishful thinking on her Beta's part. As they reached the crest of a ridge, though, she blinked and sucked in a breath.

The three dogs were gazing out over a broad plain that sloped down gently toward the Endless Lake. The sky was paling to a misty blue now as the Sun-Dog stretched and rose from his nighttime den; claws of pale golden light breached the distant horizon. Below them lay a long stretch of green grass, and right in the middle of it stood a gleaming figure.

Storm's jaw hung loose, and her heart stumbled in her chest. The creature seemed to be made of golden light, but the shape of a deer was perfectly clear. It was poised to run, yet it was gazing back intently at the dogs.

Almost as if it wants to be chased, thought Storm. Her mouth felt dry with anticipation.

"I was beginning to think you'd imagined it," she whispered to Lucky.

He gave a bark of joy, and sprang down the slope. Elegantly, the Golden Deer turned and leaped, swift and sure, into the race.

Lucky and Snap had been hunting through the night, for far longer than Storm had, and despite her dream-walk she was pulling ahead of her two companions as the Sun-Dog's shining face rose over the horizon. Ahead of her the deer still galloped, burnished like coppery Red-Leaf foliage, but Storm hesitated, glancing over her shoulder. Lucky and Snap were falling back, exhausted, and they were beginning to limp as they ran.

I can't go on chasing the deer without Lucky . . . this is his dream. With the greatest reluctance, Storm trotted to a halt, and waited for her companions to catch up.

Lucky was panting hard. "I don't think we're going to catch it tonight." There was aching regret in his voice.

"No," agreed Snap, her head hanging low with weariness. "But see where it's led us? We've been chasing it in a circle around our camp, all night." She nodded toward the first belt of trees that bordered the forest. The early light of the Sun-Dog made the green of them glow.

Storm licked her jaws thoughtfully. "Yes. We've been just beyond our home territory the whole time. Why would the deer behave like that?"

Lucky's ears were pricked high, despite his tiredness. "I think that's encouraging," he told them. "It's not the behavior of a normal deer, is it? A regular deer would just bolt. I think it's more proof—if we ever needed it—that we've found the Golden Deer."

"I don't care anymore," panted Snap, with a roll of her eyes. "I just want it to *stop*, so we can catch the thing."

"So we're not giving up?" Storm glanced from Snap to Lucky.

"Oh, no." Lucky grinned, and Snap nodded her agreement. "I feel as if I could hunt this deer till the Sun-Dog goes back to his den."

Storm hesitated. Her Beta looked tired, but there was no dimming of the fire in his eyes. "I'll tell you what I've noticed," she said slowly. "The wind has been at our backs all night. It doesn't matter which direction we've run, the wind has been with us. And yet we've been running in a circle! Do you think the Wind-Dogs are helping us?" Her tongue lolled with enthusiasm. "Because I think so. I think they want us to catch the Golden Deer, because they favor our Pack. I think they want us to have it—for your pups, Lucky!"

Lucky gazed thoughtfully after the deer, narrowing his eyes against the glare of the rising Sun-Dog. "I think you're right, Storm. Destiny and the Spirit Dogs are on our side."

"There it goes again!" Snap seemed to forget instantly about her aching limbs and lungs. She bounded toward a smear of gold on the very farthest edge of the grassy meadow. Lucky and Storm sprang after her.

With her breath back, Storm could register her surroundings, and find her bearings more exactly. *The Deer has led us almost as far as the longpaw town,* she realized. *But it can't want to go there. . . .*

And sure enough, the shimmering figure turned again, racing toward the Endless Lake. The dogs put on speed, filled with a new determination.

We're closing in on it, thought Storm, her heart leaping in her chest. *We might actually catch the Golden Deer!*

She barely noticed where she was going anymore; she was conscious only of Snap ahead of her and Lucky at her side, their muscles rippling and their fur flying in the wind of their own speed. As they crested a grassy dune, though, all three dogs came to a slithering standstill.

Down on the hard sand, the Deer was closer than ever. Storm could make out its dark shining eyes as it turned its head to watch its pursuers. It wasn't gasping for breath, and its flanks didn't heave. There wasn't a single streak of sweat on its glowing pelt.

This is no normal deer. The absolute, final certainty sent a ghostly thrill through Storm's bones.

"Wind-Dogs," Lucky murmured. He lifted his head and closed his eyes. "Help me run like the wind itself across the sand. Help me catch your Golden Deer!"

The sudden shift in the wind direction was shocking. For a fleeting heartbeat, Storm thought the Wind-Dogs had answered

Lucky's prayer; then she realized the breeze was gusting in their faces. It had taken on a new chill, and it blew grains of sand into their eyes and ears. Lucky shuddered, and took a step back, looking stunned.

And then they heard the sounds that the breeze carried.

Our camp, realized Storm with a chill. *The wind is blowing from the glade!*

And the sound it brings . . . that's the howling of dogs. Dogs crying out in grief . . .

"That's Sweet's voice!" yelped Lucky, twisting where he stood.

"It can't be." Snap's bark was full of bewilderment. "We're too far away."

"The wind's carrying it," gasped Storm.

"We have to go back!" barked Lucky. "I have to get back to Sweet!"

"Yes." Snap sprang into a run just as Lucky and Storm did. "We have to return to the camp!"

The Golden Deer forgotten, the three dogs ran, full of new and fearful energy. Storm was so driven by urgency she no longer felt her aching muscles, or the pain in her lungs. All she knew was that they had to get back to their Pack.

When the Pack is in danger, Spirit Deer can wait.

Alpha's howls were clearer and stronger than ever as they burst through the trees. Storm recognized more voices, too: Chase and Bruno, Breeze and Dart, Mickey and Thorn and Beetle. The high yelping yips of Sunshine and Daisy were instantly identifiable, and were filled with horror. The noise of baying dogs rebounded from pine trunks, seeming to come from all directions at once. It beat against Storm's eardrums, giving her legs fresh strength even as she leaped fallen logs and dead stumps. *We're coming, Packmates. We're coming. . . .*

The camp was still some distance away, though, when Lucky skidded to a halt, so abruptly that Storm crashed against his rump. Snap stumbled and stopped at their side. A swamping tide of relief was Storm's first reaction; it must have been even more overwhelming for Lucky.

Alpha stood in a small forest clearing, head tipped back, howling; but she looked unharmed, and her flanks were still rounded with pups. The other Pack members were gathered around her, their voices raised to the Sky-Dogs in grief.

Lucky shouldered through the ranks, Storm right behind him. As he came to an abrupt halt, she trotted on a pace, then two. Then one more.

Halting, Storm stared at the ground in disbelief. The body of a dog, already cold, lay like a carelessly discarded soft-hide on the forest litter. The smell of death snaked into her nostrils, and an ancient memory flared inside her skull, unwelcome: *The hollow curve of a motionless flank. Bristly hair on a dog's neck, stiff and dark with blood. Punctured holes, ragged and torn at the edges.*

No. Storm shuddered violently. This was not the Dog-Garden, and she was no pup anymore. This body was small and gray, torn with savage bites. Its throat had been ripped out.

For a moment she didn't recognize the corpse, but perhaps that was only because she didn't want to. Storm's head swam, and a twist of nausea wrenched her gut.

Whisper.

She thought her legs might give way under her. The howls of her Packmates were deafening now, throbbing painfully in her head.

What happened? Oh, Whisper. You didn't deserve this.

Her mind flailed. Was this the revenge of the foxes, or had some other creature murdered Whisper? *The culprit could still be close by!*

But . . . those are not fox bites. As Storm took a shaky pace closer to the corpse, the recognition clawed at her innards. *Close by? No, worse. The enemy could be right here among us.*

Because she knew one thing, with sickening certainty, as she stared at Whisper's cold, torn, and broken body:

Those wounds were made by a dog.

KEEP WATCH FOR

THE GATHERING DARKNESS

SURVIVORS

BOOK 2:
DEAD OF NIGHT

Darkness has struck at the heart of the Wild Pack. Whisper is dead—and Storm is certain that his wounds could only have been inflicted by another dog. Meanwhile, her dreams are troubled by shadowy visions that guide her paws through the forest while she sleeps. Can Storm trust her Packmates when she can't even trust herself?

CHAPTER ONE

In the clearing outside the Pack's camp, dogs swarmed around the edges of Storm's vision like panicking shadows, howling and yapping in grief and terror.

The weak paws of the Sun-Dog were brushing the tops of the trees, but they hadn't reached the ground. The light that filtered down to the corpse at Storm's forepaws was gray, matching the ragged fur of the dog's coat.

Only the vivid splashes of blood stood out against the dimness of the dawn.

A dog did this.

Storm sank down to her belly, staring into Whisper's lifeless eyes. His wounds were terrible. No dog could have survived them, let alone sweet, scrawny Whisper. His flank and stomach had been raked with strong claws, and his throat had been torn away.

Storm's paws rested at the edge of a patch of dark earth, almost black, where Whisper had given all his blood to the Earth-Dog.

Storm had seen dead dogs before—lots of them. She remembered their faces. Her Mother-Dog's ears had been flopped forward in sadness. Blade's pup had seemed peaceful, though his death had been anything but. Terror's upper lip had been twisted in a crazed, furious snarl, right to the end.

But Whisper's eyes were wide, his jaw slightly open, as if in surprise.

Who has done this to you?

Storm realized she was panting, shuddering as she breathed. She felt cold, but she didn't know if it was true cold or just the chill of horror.

Her Packmates were still whining and circling Whisper's body. Bruno paced anxiously back and forth, his big paws skittering across the ground, as if he was afraid to touch the earth where Whisper had died. The Pack's Omega, Sunshine, quivered at the foot of a tree, hiding her face behind a clump of grass.

Storm was vaguely aware of some dog howling, "Follow the scent, find them!" A few of the dogs crashed through the bushes and into the trees, little white Daisy and tall, scruffy Rake among them. A moment later they were joined by Mickey,

3

the black-and-white Farm Dog.

It's too late. You can't save Whisper now, Storm thought. *And you won't find his killer. He's been dead too long.* His wounds were drying, and he smelled cold. Whoever had murdered Whisper would be far away by now.

Once again, the thought hit Storm: *A dog did this to Whisper. But which dog?*

"How could this have happened?" Alpha howled, anger overtaking shock in her voice. "This is our territory! Where are the dogs who were on patrol last night?"

"I—I was, Alpha," said Thorn, stepping forward on shaking legs.

"I was leading the patrol, Alpha," said Breeze, coming to Thorn's side. She gave the young dog a reassuring nudge with her nose. Breeze's paws were steady, but when she glanced over at Whisper's body, her brown eyes were deep and dark. "We were running the border of the camp all night. Neither of us saw anything."

It takes a while to get all the way around the camp and back, Storm thought. *It would be easy to avoid the patrol, if a dog didn't want to be seen.* But to know that, the killer must have been watching the Pack and learning the Patrol Dogs' habits . . . and that meant that some dog was out there, a dog they didn't know about, and that dog had chosen to come into their territory to murder poor Whisper.

It didn't make sense.

Unless . . . that dog hadn't needed to pass the patrol at all.

Storm shook her head, as if she could dislodge the thought before it took hold. But it forced its way to the front of her mind despite her efforts. It felt like a betrayal to even consider it, but . . .

What if Whisper's killer had come from within the camp?

Storm glanced around at the other dogs, fearing and hoping at the same time that she wasn't the only one to have thought this. But the rest of the Pack was still focused on Alpha and the Patrol Dogs, who stood with their tails held low.

Alpha glared at Breeze and Thorn, her thin legs trembling with rage and the effort of standing for so long when her belly was swollen with unborn pups. "You didn't see anything. You didn't scent anything. So your patrol failed us."

Dart, Beetle, and Omega all howled in agreement and distress.

"What does this mean?" Omega whined.

Dart dipped her head, and her ears flattened to her skull. "Are our patrols useless?"

"They certainly weren't any use to Whisper," Woody said in a hollow growl.

"The whole point of having Patrol Dogs is to keep danger outside the Pack," Alpha said. She drew herself up to her full height, pricking her ears, and looked down her long nose at Moon and the other Patrol Dogs. "We need better, more frequent patrols. I want twice as many dogs on watch at all times."

Storm's panting breath caught for a moment as all eyes in the Pack turned toward Moon. She was still the lead Patrol Dog, even though Alpha had put her on High Watch as a punishment for the crime of stealing food from the prey pile. A crime Storm was certain Moon had not committed. She must have run down from the cliff at the sound of the dogs' grief. Now she sniffed the air defensively.

"We can double the patrols, Alpha," she said stiffly, "if the Patrol Dogs give up sleeping properly. With the greatest respect," she added, dipping her head in deference to Alpha's glare, "we simply don't have enough dogs, not now that we have scouts going off with the hunters every day. The Patrol Dogs have to rest sometime! Perhaps if I came off High Watch, then—"

"If our enemies do not rest, then neither will we," Alpha snapped. "And you will remain on High Watch until I say otherwise!"

Lucky stepped closer to Alpha, and she leaned against her Beta's golden flank with a grateful sigh. "Alpha is right. We must defend the Pack. And Whisper's death must be avenged," he added. "We have been attacked! We must strike back, and quickly."

Barks of agreement echoed around the clearing as one by one the Pack Dogs' ears pricked up. Bella gave her litter-brother a stern nod. Snap's lips curled back in a snarl, and Woody raked the earth beneath his claws impatiently.

Storm barked a quiet "Yes" along with the rest, but she couldn't summon up any of her Fierce Dog fury right now. Whisper's blank eyes and lifeless paws kept drawing her gaze back, stealing her attention from the Pack's rallying cries.

At least when she looked at Lucky, she felt a small spark of hope.

He has a plan! He must have an idea how we can find out who did this. She sat up attentively, waiting to hear it.

"We know who must have done this," Lucky announced. "Those mangy creatures, the foxes!"

Storm cocked her torn ear, confused. Why would he think that?

"They attacked our camp," Lucky went on, his voice rising into an angry howl. "They believe we killed one of their pups, and

7

this is their revenge! They are insane, evil . . . *not-dogs*! And this time they have gone too far. We will strike back!"

The dogs howled and their tails thudded against the earth in approval.

"Revenge for Whisper!" Breeze said, and Thorn and Beetle both yapped along with her.

"Drive them out of our territory!"

"They'll never hurt a dog again!"

Storm glanced from dog to dog, a whine vibrating in her throat, too quiet for the others to hear. Had any of these dogs actually *looked* at Whisper's wounds? Did Lucky not realize that there was no fox-scent in the clearing?

"That's right! We'll—" Lucky began, then stopped abruptly, his head snapping around to look at his mate. Alpha was nodding along with the Pack's anger, but her legs were trembling, and she blinked slowly, as if she was losing strength, and fast.

"You must get some rest," said Moon, padding over to Alpha, their arguments forgotten. "The pups need you to be still."

"The pups will be fine," said Alpha, but she didn't resist when Beta gently nudged her into a walk, steering her away toward the camp and their den.

Without their Alpha or Beta to lead the discussion, the other dogs had started to gather around Twitch, the Pack's Third Dog, barking over one another in their enthusiasm.

"We'll need to find those fiends' den if we're going to take revenge," said Bruno.

But it wasn't *the foxes. . . .*

Storm pawed the ground anxiously. She had to tell some dog— but she knew that she couldn't simply bound over to the others and contradict what their Beta had just said.

Alpha and Lucky had to be told what had really happened.

She almost couldn't bring herself to leave Whisper. Even his old Packmates had left his side now, turning away to hunt for his killer or join in the talk of revenge. Surely some dog had to stay with him? But it was Storm's duty to tell the two leaders what she'd seen, and so she cast a sad glance back at Whisper and then pushed through the undergrowth, running after them.

It took her only a couple of long strides to reach the edge of the forest and leave the shadows of the trees behind. She ran over the soft, damp grass with the early light of the Sun-Dog gleaming down on her back. The Wind-Dogs carried the faint scent of the Endless Lake over the cliffs to the high, sunlit camp where the Pack had made their home.

Alpha and Lucky weren't moving very fast, hampered by

the swift-dog's tiredness and the extra weight of their pups, and Storm caught up with them as they passed the small pond just outside the camp.

"Alpha! Beta, wait," she barked. With all the dogs out in the forest, the place was eerily quiet, and her bark seemed louder than she'd meant it to. A small bird that had been perched by the edge of the still water startled and flew away. The two older dogs paused.

"What's the matter, Storm? Has something happened?" Lucky asked.

"I—I wanted to talk to you about Whisper."

"Alpha must get some rest." Lucky shook his head. "Can it wait until I get back?"

"I'm all right, Lucky," said Alpha, and gave him an affection-ate nudge with the top of her head. "Why don't you stay and talk to Storm? I can get myself to the den."

"Are you sure?" Lucky said, looking around, as if to search for foxes hiding in the long grass by the pond.

"Are you challenging your Alpha?" his mate teased. "I can walk a few steps by myself. Stay with Storm." She turned her back on him and walked, slowly but with dignity, up the slope toward the den. Lucky kept his eyes fixed on her, watching every step she took until she was out of sight. Storm shifted from paw to paw, feeling a strange prickle of impatience as she waited for her Beta to give her his attention. Her resolve wavered—she suspected he wasn't going to like what she had to say, and it would be so easy to turn around and join the others. . . .

No, I have to tell him!

"I don't think the foxes killed Whisper," Storm blurted out. Lucky's head whipped around, and he fixed her with a wide-eyed stare.

"Of course they did. They believe we killed their pup. That's all the motive they would need. . . ."

"But there was no scent, Lucky! Foxes smell terrible, and there was no scent on Whisper's body except for dogs and . . . and blood."

Lucky's brows drew together, and he stared over Storm's shoulder, back toward the forest, for a long moment. Then he shook his head. "Whisper's body was cold. It must have been there for some time before the patrol stumbled on it—the fox-scents could have faded in that time."

"I don't think so," Storm pressed. "And even if they had, I'm *sure* we would have smelled them in the forest! The patrols didn't report scenting foxes, and I didn't smell any as we came in from the hunt . . . did you?"

Lucky kept on staring toward the forest and didn't answer. Storm guessed he didn't remember—she couldn't blame him for being distracted, when they'd been following the sound of Alpha howling in grief and pain.

"Anyway," she went on, "foxes' jaws are small. Their claws aren't very strong. Come back and look again, you'll see it too. I think Whisper was killed by a dog."

At that, Lucky's eyes snapped back to focus on Storm. "What? You think the Fierce Dogs did this?" he snarled. Storm's ears pulled back, and she looked away. "Or some other bad dog from outside the Pack?" Lucky added quickly.

Storm didn't meet his eyes. He'd tried to cover it, but Lucky's thoughts had gone straight to her birth Pack, to dogs like her and Arrow.

"I don't know," she said quietly. "I didn't smell any unfamiliar dog scents, but . . ."

Lucky shook his head. "Well, then what dog could have killed him? Storm, I know you're upset, but that's enough." He turned away. "There are no dogs around here who would attack our Pack—we would have met them before. Whisper must have been killed by the foxes."

"But Beta, the scent—"

"Foxes are cunning creatures," Lucky barked. "They must have covered their scent somehow. And as for the size of their jaws, foxes come in all sizes, just like dogs. That proves nothing."

No, that's not right. I'm sure the bite marks are wrong for a fox. . . . A vision of Whisper's bloodied throat flashed before Storm's eyes. She had to make sure Lucky understood her fear, even if the thought was so dark she could barely allow herself to think it. "Beta," she said again, "what if some dog in our Pack—"

"Quiet, pup!" Lucky's eyes flashed angrily, and Storm shifted back on her paws. "Stop this nonsense, right now. I know it's hard to see something like this happen to a good dog like Whisper. It's hard for the whole Pack. That's why I need you to promise me you won't go bothering the other dogs with this . . . this ridiculous theory!"

Less ridiculous than pinning it on the foxes, Storm thought. *Whether you can face it or not.* But she kept quiet, her head low, as Lucky paced back and forth in front of her, scattering the dew drops with his swishing tail.

"The Pack is under attack, Storm, do you understand that?" Lucky barked. "We need to be strong right now—for Alpha, and for the pups, and for every dog. If you start accusing Pack Dogs of murdering one of our own, there will be panic, and they'll turn on each other. They'll turn on *you*, most likely!" Lucky's voice became softer, but no less certain. "The foxes killed Whisper, Storm. I won't hear another word about it."

Without even waiting for Storm to reply, he turned and hurried after Alpha toward their den.

Storm stared after him, unease forming a hot ball in her stomach.

What do I do now?

ERIN HUNTER

is inspired by a fascination with the ferocity of the natural world. As well as having great respect for nature in all its forms, Erin enjoys creating rich, mythical explanations for animal behavior. She is also the author of the bestselling Warriors and Seekers series.

Visit the Packs online and chat on Survivors message boards at www.survivorsdogs.com!

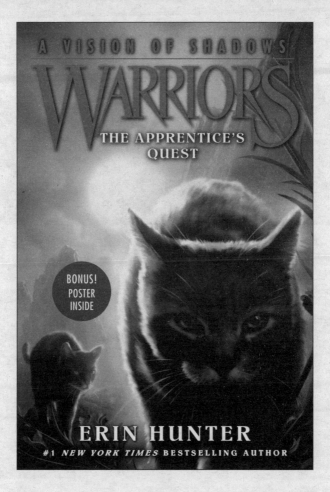

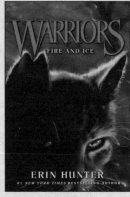

WARRIORS: THE NEW PROPHECY

In the second series, follow the next generation of heroic cats as they set off on a quest to save the Clans from destruction.

HARPER
An Imprint of HarperCollinsPublishers

www.warriorcats.com

WARRIORS: POWER OF THREE

In the third series, Firestar's grandchildren begin their training as warrior cats. Prophecy foretells that they will hold more power than any cats before them.

HARPER
An Imprint of HarperCollinsPublishers

www.warriorcats.com

WARRIORS: OMEN OF THE STARS

1

2

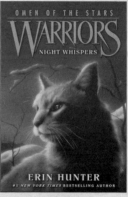

3

4

5

6

In the fourth series, find out which ThunderClan
apprentice will complete the prophecy.

HARPER
An Imprint of HarperCollinsPublishers

WARRIORS: DAWN OF THE CLANS

THE SUN TRAIL

ERIN HUNTER

#1 *NEW YORK TIMES* BESTSELLING AUTHOR

THUNDER RISING

ERIN HUNTER

#1 *NEW YORK TIMES* BESTSELLING AUTHOR

THE FIRST BATTLE

ERIN HUNTER

#1 *NEW YORK TIMES* BESTSELLING AUTHOR

THE BLAZING STAR

ERIN HUNTER

#1 *NEW YORK TIMES* BESTSELLING AUTHOR

A FOREST DIVIDED

ERIN HUNTER

#1 *NEW YORK TIMES* BESTSELLING AUTHOR

PATH OF STARS

ERIN HUNTER

#1 *NEW YORK TIMES* BESTSELLING AUTHOR

In this prequel series,
discover how the warrior Clans came to be.

HARPER
An Imprint of HarperCollinsPublishers

www.warriorcats.com

WARRIORS: SUPER EDITIONS

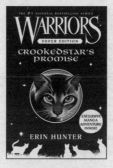

These extra-long, stand-alone adventures will take you deep inside each of the Clans with thrilling tales featuring the most legendary warrior cats.

HARPER
An Imprint of HarperCollinsPublishers

www.warriorcats.com

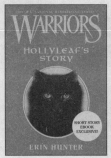

SURVIVORS: THE GATHERING DARKNESS

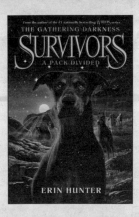

In the **second series**, tensions are rising within the pack.

SURVIVORS: BONUS STORIES

Download the three separate ebook novellas or read them in one paperback bind-up!

HARPER
An Imprint of HarperCollinsPublishers

www.survivorsdogs.com

ALSO BY ERIN HUNTER:
SURVIVORS

SURVIVORS: THE ORIGINAL SERIES

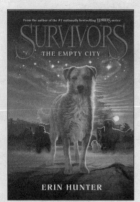

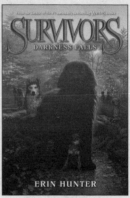

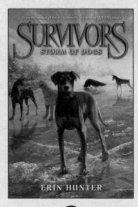

The time has come for dogs to rule the wild.

HARPER
An Imprint of HarperCollinsPublishers

www.survivorsdogs.com